The Cynic Fantasy

written by Studio 136

Diana Gaffner
Paige Saraga
Mia Seshadri
Tallulah Echtenkamp

Under the direction of JGo
and Written Out Loud Studios

Book jacket design by Naomi Giddings

ISBN 978-1-300-95458-3

Dedicated to Mr. Hilpert, Mr. Winston and
Mr. Fisher for being amazing teachers and
inspiring me to write. Thanks in addition to my
family, who has been wonderfully supportive.
-Diana

Dedicated to Anita Macfarlane, Marie-jose
Souche and the Saraga /Gampel family. Thank
you all for helping me feel the inspiration to write.
-Paige

Dedicated to all of my super cool teachers that
have inspired me to write stories.
-Mia

Dedicated to my very inspiring family and friends
who have inspired me to write.
-Tallulah

Contents

"We didn't realize we were making memories, we just knew we were having fun."
-Winnie the Pooh

Chapter 1

The end of the refectory table was shrouded in light. Willow sat at the end of the table, her hair flooded in front of her face. She distanced herself from her family as much as she could. She hated spending time with them. They didn't laugh or cry; they didn't live. For all Willow knew, her aunt could be a robot. Maybe that's why she only saw her once a month. She was getting oiled and re-wired between their meetups.

The adults were chatting and eating, talking about things of little meaning to them. None of them cared how the weather was, and none of them cared how the kids were doing. All they cared about was having status, riches and being "normal." Whatever that meant. The Fallons lived by many rules, but the most prominent one was "every man for themself."

Now, what does a Fallon do when someone in their group does not follow these rules? They forget them, push them out of their lives, even the children. They are outcast and left out, though there's not much to be left out of. The family is barely together. For the children, being a Fallon means a house, food, high expectations and a grey, boring life.

"Willow!" Aunt Alice exclaimed in a high pitched voice. She was tall and thin, and she wore a short red dress that accentuated her curves but hid them with a black fluffy fur coat. Her make up masked her face, Willow remembered seeing her once without makeup. She had stumbled into the guest room, forgetting about her aunt who was sleeping there. Aunt Alice was truly beautiful, she had freckles dotted across her nose. A birthmark as well, shaped like Africa. It was just above her left cheekbone. Willow remembered her aunt's screams when she walked in, her hands masking her face. Willow wanted to tell her how beautiful she was, but she knew that Aunt Alice wouldn't let her. She also knew that Aunt Alice wouldn't let herself believe Willow either.

Willow let her mind wander into a new world, a world where her aunt was a passionate warrior. *Her stare made the toughest of monsters whimper. She was in a raging battle, facing a massive, bulky man in iron armour. He couldn't be human, seeing he was past 9 feet tall. She herself had no makeup on, she wore nothing more for armour than a leather vest with a thin layer of flexible metal inside so she could stay light on her feet. The hidden warrior was known for her amazing dodges*

3

and risky attacks, armour would slow her down. Her face was held low to the ground.

"Hmmm, so this is the hidden warrior I've heard so much about," the man chuckled in a low voice.

"I believe I am," said Alice with confidence. Her jagged hair blew in the wind. Bloodied bodies and abandoned weapons laid all around the field.

"I see you've gotten past my men. Impressive," he growled, "now how about trying to get through me?" The man jumped towards Alice as the image faded out of Willow's mind. She was snapped back to reality by the sound of Aunt Alice's shrill voice.

"Get your head out of the clouds and pay attention!" she shrieked, her nose was up in the air. "Samuel, Kathy, you must do something about that child!" She thrust her finger towards Willow. "She's always dreaming, and we all know that dreamers get nowhere," she said angrily.

"Sorry Aunt Alice," Willow mumbled. She fiddled with her fingers under the desk. Willow longed to be back at school, where she could see her friend, Griffin, again. He was one of the only people in her life who would let her share the worlds inside her head with him. They would talk for hours about dragons and forested villages inhabited by elves, fauns, dwarfs and warriors. He would sit and listen to her, she would listen to him. They both preferred these daydreams over their daily lives. Neither had ever really seen the world outside of their school and their homes. There were the people at school and the people at home, that was it. So they weren't really ones to talk.

Willow lived by a single story of the outside world: it is cruel, foreboding, and not a place one wants to need help in, because you'll never receive it. No one who deserves a break gets one. Anyone who needs a light in life is left in darkness. Willow assumed that of the outside world, because that is what she had learned from her family. She always thought that outside of her school, good was only an ideal, not a reality. Willow knew that the outside world was harsh although she had never been anywhere except boarding school and her small valley town, Wood Creek.

"Well, Willow will never end up a big figure in the cheese industry like me if she doesn't get her head out of the clouds!" said Uncle David. He was greasy and smelly, and you could always see some sort of food stain on his painfully small shirt. He had one of the largest pot bellies you have ever seen. Willow would never want to be anything like him. He lived in Baltimore and probably was the cause of how bad the city smelled. He ran a massive cheese production plant and was obsessed with the stuff. Uncle David is the only person you will ever see with several jars of pickled cheese. No one in the family liked him, but they respected him enough.

Willow and her family sat in silence for a bit longer, but this was tradition. Stiff silence. This was life, and her family wondered why she was always imagining a different one.

Chapter 2

"Willow! Get in the car!" Willow's mom, Kathy Fallon, yelled from out front. Only one more night of this until Willow would be heading back to school, away from her controlling family.

"I've just got to finish some work!" She protested.

"That school gives you way too much homework over break. Don't they know you are here to spend time with your family? There's a playground and I need to pick something up at the store. Get in the car!" Kathy repeated, and Willow rolled her eyes before getting in the car.

"I'm 14, Mom. I need to do some work, and at the moment, I don't really have time to play on a playground, and I don't want to either."

"Well, that's where we are going, and I am not leaving you at home. You need to get out sometimes. When you aren't at school, you spend all your time in your room doing work *for* school." Kathy had never been to Willow's school. She skipped every parent visiting day, every parent-teacher conference. She would rather Willow go to school in Wood Creek instead of at a boarding school four hours away. She was only there because of the status of Apol-lodorus Academy. Any opportunity the Fallon family had to move up in the social hierarchy they would take. To protest the school, however, she never visited at all.

"Fine. I need to remind Finn to pick me up anyway." Willow got into the car, squished with her relatives.

The family arrived at the playground after an awkward car ride. At least Willow had gotten a seat next to her Grandma. She didn't reek of rotten cheese like her uncle did.

Willow's parents and her grandmother dropped her off at the park while they continued down the road to find a parking spot. Happy to get out of the car, Willow walked towards the swings. Among other things, Kathy hated swings. She always thought Willow was going to fall and hurt herself. She forced her daughter to be on a playground, but hated it when Willow actually found some fun in the experience. Parents were so strange some-times, especially Willow's. Willow kicked her legs, and she started swinging.

The grass below her turned to lava, and she kicked higher to make sure she didn't fall into the steaming pit below her. She got higher and swerved as a dragon swooped at her. She pumped her legs one more time before she jumped to the other side of the volcano, and onto the ground. The impact snapped her back to reality, and she rubbed her leg. Willow's mom whipped around from where she stood, helping Willow's grandmother out of the car. Kathy had seemingly forgotten about Grandma Grant as she began to yell.

"Willow Fallon! You don't need to dive off the swings." Kathy had turned at the exact time she fell. Time had some certain vendetta against Willow, she was sure.

"I was just having some fun!" Willow exclaimed, leaving out the details of her adventures. Willow's mother had made it quite clear that she was not pleased with Willow's "childlike" behavior.

"I told you to stop imagining these things! There are no lava, dragons, unicorns, or ocean monsters. There never have been, and there never will be. Someday, you will really hurt yourself!" If Willow's mother could do only one thing with her life, it would be to make Willow a normal, presentable teenager, with a weak and boring mind.

"But I didn't," Willow protested.

"But you will!"

"But I didn't."

"But you will!"

"But I didn't!"

"Willow. Someday you will hurt yourself and you can not blame me because it will be your fault," Willow's mom ended the conversation.

Kathy had never accepted Willow's wild imagination. It was true that for the age of 14, she was extraordinarily creative and imaginative, but it wasn't at all bad. It just got slightly out of hand sometimes. Maybe if she could express it at home, it wouldn't be cooped up. A dragon wouldn't burn down a town if it was able to fly freely. Willow had learned that; the hard way, of course. Everything always had to be done the hard way when it came to dragons. The hard way, as in mother dragons being overly protective over her eggs. Willow had created a million scenarios in her mind about trying to get a dragon egg for herself, thinking it would be great to have a dragon companion. But, mother dragons always did the same thing, and Willow barely made it out of each imaginary scenario not being burnt to a crisp.

Unfortunately, Willow was not a dragon and didn't live in a world where they did exist. So for the time being, she stuck to visits to the butcher's shop and imagining other worlds in her head, or with Griffin. Worlds other than the small, hopeless case of Wood Creek.

Wood Creek was a small valley town. A town with a small population and people with tiny imaginations. People who thrived on routine. Every day was a repetition. Nothing ever happened in the town of Wood Creek. The people were too bleak for anything to happen. Willow couldn't wait to get out of there and never look back. Even now, Willow hated school breaks, the only time of the year she was home, instead of at Apollodorus Academy, the boarding school she went to. Thanksgiving break was even worse, since apparently that meant the cheese market thrived.

Willow's mother ushered her and Grandma Grant over to the sidewalk. They searched down the marketplace of town, trying to find the store that would suit their needs. They walked by the butcher's shop, seeing the butcher standing outside. He had a smoky grey beard and one of the widest smiles she had ever seen. He had a low cheery voice and a kindness that seemed uncharacteristic for his profession. He loved letting people taste his food, if not for the satisfaction of seeing the delight on their faces then out of the kindness in his heart. If you met him on the sidewalk or at a park you would never assume his profession.

With blood stained gloves and apron, he waved at the Fallons from the store as they walked by slowly. Willow's mom humphed and lifted her nose up higher. Her father paid no attention to the cheery man.

When Willow had first met him, she thought he was a viking. Turns out he just slaughtered animals for a living. Even though she knew that the butcher was kind and wouldn't actually kill her, she was still a little scared of him.

They passed by the seamstress, an old woman who was fiddling away with her yarn and needles at the front. She was about as old as a fossil, but she gave out lovely cookies. Everyone in Wood Creek gave each other food, except for Willow's family. Willow's parents would rather throw out food than give it to the other people in her town. They lived with a set of morals that were foreign to Willow. If the Fallons couldn't have it, then nobody else could either. They had to be on top, and they had to have power.

It was late fall, and the valley was dotted with dandelions. Willow knew that she could make a lot of money from a weed pulling business if she was ever allowed to have a job, or even interact with the citizens of Wood Creek. The only time she could do so is when one of them had to drive her to boarding school. With her unforgiving and rude family, rarely anyone ever wanted to do it. Except Finn, the butcher. He would do it.

The drive from the valley to Apollodorus Academy was bumpy due to the gravel path. The further you got from the town, the less littered the road was with trash and roadkill. The bumpiness of the gravel paths made up for the lack of roadkill to run over. Apollodorus was an hour outside of the city, in the middle of nowhere. The masses of land that stretched on for miles and miles seemed to belong solely to the school.

Willow couldn't help but look forward to the day being over. She would be able to go back to Apollodorus Academy, and she could see Griffin again. Realizing that her family had stopped in a store, Willow closed her eyes. Beneath her eyelids she saw the streaming rivers on campus. The students around the campfires, the seven classroom buildings, the three dorm buildings. She saw the kids studying outside on the grass. When Willow closed her eyes, she could go anywhere. Willow was snapped back to reality as the butcher's hearty laugh sounded down the street. She sighed as he waved off a couple who had just bought some meat. Before she could once again travel to her imagination, Willow's family walked by.

"Time to go, Willow. We've got all we need for dinner tonight," Willow's father put a meaty hand on her shoulder and guided her over to the car. Frustrated, Willow shoved his hand off of her shoulder.

"One second, Dad!" Before he could pull her back, Willow ran over to the butcher's shop. "Hey, Finn! Don't forget that I've got to get to boarding school tomorrow. Could you drive me up at 7:00 tomorrow morning?" Finn wiped his hands on his aprons and smiled brightly at her.

"Ah, that time already? Course, I'll be there at 7:00, don't worry." He went back to his meat as Willow's father beckoned her over to the car.

"Okay, see you then!" Willow waved over her shoulder as she ran to her family. As she neared the car, her father tapped his leg impatiently.

"You're too old for playgrounds, but you're not old enough to stop getting caught up in daydreams. Get in the car, next to your uncle." Willow rolled her eyes at the punishment and slid in next to her uncle. He reeked of rotten cheese and sweat, but she supposed family was family. He smiled crookedly at Willow, and offered a piece of cheese, which Willow politely declined. She closed her eyes, preparing for the forty five minute drive back to her house.

Willow must've fallen asleep on the way back -- a fact she was quite glad about. She preferred sleep to hearing her family talk about the villagers behind their back. Willow stumbled out of the car and out in front of the large wooden house. It was unnecessarily large, and her family did not deserve nor need the amount of space they had. After all, it wasn't like they were accepting visitors. No, the Fallon family would never open up their doors to other people.

Each person walked through the heavy doors, letting the door shut behind them. Willow was just about to walk through the door behind her uncle, but the door slammed in her face. Willow scoffed and marveled in her family's stupidity before opening the door. She walked through the doors and was greeted by the smell of dinner being started. It didn't have a good smell. Somehow, Willow's family had already managed to burn something, and it hadn't even been five minutes since they got home. Her family may be talented with cheese, but it was ill-advised to give them any control over other foods.

"Willow, come help with the food!" Her mother shouted after the door had shut behind her. More interaction with her mother? No thanks. Besides, she had homework to do.

"I'll come down later, Mom. I've got to finish a paper for English class." Willow knew it was the wrong thing to say when her mom whipped around, a stern look in her eyes.

"Of course they assign you work on your break when you get to come home with us!" Kathy spoke threateningly with a ladle in her hand. While the image itself wasn't very frightening, Willow knew that any talk about school while she was home would work her mother into a fit.

"On second thought, I can probably do the home-work later. What do you need me to prepare for dinner?" If Willow couldn't skip out on cooking, she might as well try to help salvage the meal. Her mother pointed to the meat on the counter. Willow picked it up squeamishly and placed it next to where all the spices were. Her mother knew she hated working with meat, but it seemed that she was always the one to prepare it. Willow never complained about it, and not just because complaining would only make her parents angry. Finn had been trying to teach her how to work with meat, though she hadn't been making much progress. She wanted to make him proud of her-- to have someone be proud of her.

Willow mindlessly prepared the meat, tuning out the chatter of her family around her. At some point, she was sure they were talking about how terrible Apollodorus Academy was. If it wasn't the homework, it was the teachers. If it wasn't the teachers, it was the tests. No matter what, they found something to complain about.

Willow had to put effort into ignoring their words. If they said one more bad thing about the place she called home, Willow was sure she would finally start an argument. And if that happened? Well, if that happened, Willow would probably never be returning to Apollodorus Academy. Instead, Willow kept her insults to herself to use for another time.

After the meal had been prepared, Willow sat down at the dining table. A chandelier loomed above the table, looking far too heavy for the wooden roof it was connected to. Willow was secretly terrified that it would fall on her, but she didn't dare tell her family her opinions on their carefully picked furniture.

Her father came over to the table with a steaming plate of food. He had no oven mitts on. His fingers were so calloused that the heat didn't affect him. The food smelled surprisingly good tonight, but the smell quickly turned sour as Willow's family sat around her at the table. There was rarely a quiet moment in the household. This held true for dinnertime, too. The family would speak with food in their mouths, and if they were particularly passionate, they would spit bits of food into the air. This happened most frequently when they argued about the cheese stocks.

Willow nodded at appropriate times, laughed at others. But soon, she was finished with her food, and she sat in boredom at the dining table. Inhaling deeply, Willow closed her eyes. *The booming laughter around her turned into a bird's chorus. The oven top that her mother had forgotten to turn off became a dragon's breath. Trees rustled around her, and for a moment she was back at Apollodorus Academy with Griffin.* The moment was quickly snatched away as her Uncle David turned all the attention her way.

"So Willow, I hear the school is loadin' you up on work?" Uncle David asked. Willow squirmed under the attention that was now directed at her. It had been a simple enough question, but Willow knew they were testing her. One wrong word, and she'd be out of Apollodorus. Her uncle, who she knew wanted her to become a carbon copy of him when she was older, was always looking for more reasons to take her out of Apollodorus Academy.

"It's not terrible, actually. My teachers are all very understanding." Willow spoke formally. Facts, no opinions. She couldn't let something that could be possibly "offensive" slip through.

"Oh, go on! Tell her already!" Aunt Alice shouted in her nasally voice. Willow's heart skipped a beat. Her leg tapped fiercely, and her fingers drummed against the table top. It was the only thing other than her imagination that she could not control while she was around her family.

"Tell me what?" Willow asked, hoping she didn't sound as nervous as she was. Nobody spoke up, so Aunt Alice took the lead.

"Takin' you out of that damned school. Too much work, not a good enough education." Her family all grunted and nodded in agreement.

"What?" Willow's voice was deathly quiet. Even her incompetent family knew enough to be frightened by the glare Willow was giving them. She had tried *so* hard. Every single thing she had agreed to was all to stay at Apollodorus Academy. Every lie she had told, every truth she had held back. Did it mean nothing to her family that she was sacrificing her personality every time she was around them? "No. There must be something I can do." Willow began to panic. She watched as her family exchanged nervous glances with each other, deciding her future without even saying a word.

"Maybe she could get a scholarship?" Grandma Grant suggested in a frail voice. Willow's father shot Grandma Grant a stern look. It was obvious that the family had not discussed the idea of a scholarship before dinner. Willow was thankful for Grandma Grant at that moment.

"Mom, I'm not so sure about that," Willow's father spoke to Grandma Grant slowly, as if he was trying to get her to understand some secret message. Grandma Grant didn't catch any of the signals and continued rambling on.

"Well why not? Means we don't have to pay any money, and our Willow will be working harder than ever. It sounds like a win-win to me!" Grandma Grant laughed, proud of herself for coming up with such a grand idea. Before her father could interject, Willow pitched in.

"I think that would work! I would work really, really hard on the scholarship, and then you'll be getting your money's worth without even paying." Willow attempted to be convincing. As she saw the looks pass over her family's face, actually considering the idea, Willow silently thanked Mx. Wilde, her English teacher, for all of the public speaking skills she had developed. She was terrible at it in class, but she was glad that her skills chose to shine through at the dinner table.

Willow was terrified about the scholarship. She hadn't ever looked into one. Pulling her out of Apollodorus Academy was always just a threat, not something that would actually happen. Pulling her out had always been the sword dangling over her head, waiting for someone to cut the rope. *But they don't have anything over me anymore,* Willow thought wickedly. They couldn't do anything more to hurt her.

"Fine! She can do a scholarship, fine." Willow's father gave in. If her father ever had any weakness whatsoever, it was his mother. Grandma Grant smiled smugly, and she sat further back in her chair.

"Great! Who's ready for dessert?" Grandma Grant screeched her chair out from under her as if she hadn't just determined Willow's whole future. The rest of the family pushed their chairs out of the way, and the remains of the meal were thrown wastefully into the garbage and forgotten. The conversation moved back to cheese stocks, which apparently were more interesting than Willow's life.

Willow attempted to seize the opportunity to retire to her room. It was only 8:30, but she felt incredibly drained. Somehow she managed to escape before dessert without protest from her family. She hadn't wanted to spend a second more with them. Any more time and they could twist and bend her future into the mold of their choice. Willow wasn't going to give them that chance. While normally she would use her time alone to conjure up dragons in her mind, Willow wanted to travel into the world of dreams. It wasn't so different from the world of imagination. Both had a way of proving the impossible possible. Willow doubted that even a dream could take her away from the daunting scholarship that stood in the way of Apollodorus Academy.

As Willow's head hit the pillow, she did travel to the world of dreams. She supposed that's what happens when other people fall asleep too. Nobody could suppress a dream. Unlike imagination, dreams were wild and untamed. It was unpredictable and exhilarating. Everything that Willow could hope for. Though on other nights, like the one tonight, Willow's dreams were nothing more than a blanket of stars above her. They still had stories, just not her own. They pulled her into hopes and dreams that were foreign to her, but just as meaningful. Like someone reading her a story, lulling her to sleep...

Chapter 3

When Willow woke up, the rhythmic ticking of the clock signalled that the time had just passed 4:00 A.M. The house was silent and sleeping. Light had just barely cracked through the nighttime sky, mixing the twinkling stars with the orange-ish hues slowly creeping into the sheet of dark blue above her. Willow carefully pushed her blanket from on top of her, making sure not to shift on the bed. She stepped on to the floorboards, picking out the ones she knew wouldn't creak. Willow's cleanly washed school uniform sat folded on her dresser. Somehow the uniform made Willow feel free. It felt like an act of rebellion against her family. It made her unique. Whatever happened, Willow refused to lose that.

Putting on the familiar suit and tie, Willow readied herself for school. Finn wouldn't be there for another couple of hours, but that gave her time to think. She wasn't entirely sure she wanted time for her thoughts to swarm her mind, knowing what she might think of, but it would be worth it. Willow walked over to where her window was. She pressed her hand on it, feeling the cool air, before cracking it open and stepping out onto the roof. Just outside her room was an overhang. Willow wasn't entirely sure if it was safe, but nobody bothered her there. Her legs dangled over the edge, and she became lost in thought, taken away from the struggles of reality.

Willow stared into the distance. The plain valley was covered in a blanket of leaves and green bushes, and grassy patches dotted the valley. It was slightly windy. Just cold enough that she didn't have to wear a sweatshirt, but she wasn't boiling from the heat. She could feel the hairs on her arms rising and the occasional drop of water splashing against her cool skin from morning mist. Below, the entire population of Wood Creek was asleep. The small town nestled into the base of the valley.

The wind cooed and whispered around the valley, hushing the entire place. It could be telling her to sleep, seeing as it was 5:00 A.M, but Willow couldn't bear missing her favourite weather. Her tie flowed in the wind. The entire sight was calming, and she felt some sort of power. She could break the silence. She wanted to be there to sing the day into life. She could have control for once. Control over how her day would go, and her parents could do nothing to stop her. The scholarship couldn't bother her there. She was untouchable. Willow could easily think of song lyrics or poem lyrics. "The-" she let her mouth hang open for a few seconds before realizing she couldn't think of any words. She desperately searched for the lyrics in her head but she found nothing.

The sun started to rise, and she had missed her chance. Quietly, she sneaked back into the house. Willow walked downstairs and waited for her parents to wake up. She pondered nervously, pacing back and forth in front of the entrance of the house. Her shoes tapped against the dark oak, surely leaving marks. She was probably fine. She had to be fine. Her creativity was her whole world. It was probably just too early in the morning, or she was just too tired. She tried to sing again, but the tune wasn't hers. It was stolen. Mimicked from something she had heard before. She didn't copy, she created.

Willow's bag swung against her back every time she paced, making her go faster. She worked herself into a stressful trance. Wondering if she was having an off day, or if what she used to keep herself going everyday was gone. Wondering if the only thing that might let her stay at Apollodorus Academy disappeared. Surely she could get a scholarship off *something*.

Willow realized she knew nothing about scholarships, and she would have to ask someone. Asking someone would just make it more real. She worked herself up, getting more and more anxious until she wanted to scream.

Suddenly, there was a loud knock on the door that made her jump. Her uncle had woken up at the sound, and he slowly walked down the stairs to stand behind her.

Willow opened the door, and there she met Finn. In his hand he held a tray of cookies. His cooking mitts were colorfully patterned and a bit messy from years of handling.

"Hello, Willow! Are you ready to go? Got here a few minutes early, just to make sure I wasn't late. If you need a few more minutes I could wait outside?" Finn offered kindly. Willow snapped out of her trance-like behavior at his words, and nodded her head. She was having an off day. How could someone lose their imagination? Especially not Willow. Yes. She was having an off day.

"No, no you're right on time. Let me go grab my bag." Willow dodged past her uncle and his bitter cup of coffee before realizing that the bag still sat securely on her shoulders. Finn laughed as Willow made the realization, and he gestured her through the door.

"Well come now then." He grinned widely. How he could be this happy while helping the rudest family in Wood Creek was a mystery to Willow.

Willow walked out of the door without a goodbye. Her parents would be mad, but she didn't care. As Finn closed the door behind him, he gave a quick tip of his hat to Willow's uncle before they were on their way.

Finn ran down the steps to catch up with Willow, jostling the tray of cookies, and he clapped Willow on the back. Surprised, she yelped, before breaking into laughter and grabbing a still-warm cookie from the tray. Willow decided that she wouldn't tell Finn about the scholarship. She could forget about it for a moment in the car, and she could just talk to Finn like she always had before when he would drive her. The two stepped into the car and began the long drive.

"Finn," Willow thoughtfully munched on a cookie. "Finn, did you ever have a best friend at my age?" Willow stared through the windshield, watching as the road raced by under them.

"A best friend, eh? Well, how old are you again?" Finn drove the wheel with one hand, his body slightly tilted to look at Willow. It wasn't the safest way of driving, but then again, there were rarely cars on the small town road.

"I'm fourteen, going on fifteen soon." Willow nodded as if she had just said something very important.

"Fourteen. Fourteen's a good age. One day, when you're my age, you'll look back on being fourteen. Don't you forget that. Gosh, I remember being fourteen like it was just yesterday! Now that you mention it, I did have a best friend. Can't quite remember their name though..." Finn looked puzzled as he attempted to recall his friend's name. Willow shuddered at the thought of one day forgetting Griffin's name. *It's a possibility, now that you're going to be taken out of Apollodorus Academy,* Willow's thoughts tugged at her mind.

"Well I have a best friend!" Willow declared. "His name is Griffin." Finn smiled proudly. He wasn't Willow's related family, but he sure cared a lot more about her than anyone she was actually related to did.

"Go on! Tell me about him." Willow twisted in her seat to face Finn.

"Well you see, Griffin and I met at Apollodorus. He's in my year. We met in the forest one day. With the dragons." Willow grabbed another cookie, the melted chocolate spreading over her fingers. "They aren't real dragons. Just imaginary ones. But they're fun to play with. Anyways, Griffin has this light brown hair. And he always wears the same shoes. I swear, he has no other pair!" Willow laughed as if it was an inside joke. "They're just like your shoes, Finn!" Finn gasped in mock surprise, and he gestured down to his muddied sneakers.

"Your best friend has shoes like mine? What an honor." Willow smirked, her eyes lightening with the bright sky.

"It is an honor! We might even crown you a knight. In our kingdom, of course." Willow rolled her eyes. "The *imaginary* kingdom." Finn laughed, shaking the car.

"How old did you say you were again?" Finn shook his head in amusement.

"Fourteen." Willow smiled proudly.

"Fourteen's a good age." Finn repeated, picked up a cookie, and lost himself in his thoughts, trying to dig up memories of when he was fourteen. Surprising himself, he found none. The two sat the rest of the ride in uncharacteristic silence, watching the trees blur into each other.

Finn was a good driver. Better than Grandma Grant, who drove like a sloth, or a turtle. And much better than the older teenagers and people in their twenties in town. They drove like they were escaping a crime scene. Finn drove at a good pace, and he made even better cookies than the old seamstress. Willow kept eating the cookies, until there were only four left. She would give the rest to Griffin. Griffin loved Finn's cookies, almost as much as he loved his sneakers.

Eventually, the car arrived outside of Apollodorus Academy. Throughout the course of the ride the sun had been pulled into the sky. Willow wondered if someone pulled it around the world, bringing morning to various countries. Maybe it was just a natural phenomenon that could be explained by science. Apparently science could explain anything. Maybe one day science would explain why Willow had to move to the town of Wood Creek.

As Willow opened the car door, all thoughts of Wood Creek were lost. They were replaced by the beauty of the vast campus that Willow happily called home. Even though Willow had been going to the same school for years, it seemed even more beautiful to her than it ever had. The cobbled paths from building to building made the school feel like a town. Before setting off to the Dining Hall (where the students checked back into campus for lunch on Sunday), Willow said a quick good-bye to Finn.

"Thanks for the drive, Finn!" Willow started off, but Finn's voice stopped her in her tracks.

"Is someone driving you home next break? I'd be happy to bring you if you'd like." Finn had almost forgotten to offer. He wasn't sure whether or not Willow had already made plans, but he knew that the Fallon family was reluctant to make plans with the rest of town.

"I'm not sure if anyone's driving me, but I'd love to drive with you again next break!" *If there is a next break...* Willow hadn't wanted to acknowledge that it might be her last time on the drive to Apollodorus Academy.

Finn grinned broadly. Willow greatly enjoyed his company through the long drives to school.

"I've got to go. Thanks again!" Willow sprinted off, waving to him over her shoulder. Finn waited outside until he saw her safely enter the building, like a parent would, and then repositioned himself heavily in his seat.

"Wouldn't it be great to be fourteen again?" Finn spoke to himself as he turned the car back on and turned the radio up. It was an older song -- one of the big hits from when he was in high school. The song style had certainly changed over the years. Songwriters no longer wrote about what they were feeling, or what they felt was important. Every song was the same, no original stories. Finn silently asked himself why he had stopped listening to the music of his childhood. Was it because it was outdated? Was it because others were listening to different music? If there's one thing Finn knew about himself, it was that he didn't change himself to fit others expectations. But now, he was beginning to wonder if even that was true. He let his anxiety be blared out by the noise.

Meanwhile, Willow walked into the dining hall, unaware of Finn's thoughts, her own racing to the front of her mind. It was already packed full of students and very loud. If Griffin and Willow didn't have a designated meet spot, Willow didn't think she would ever be able to find him. But they were prepared, and Willow beelined over to the corner bench where Griffin sat. In the spur of the moment decision, Willow decided that as far as Griffin would be concerned, nothing had happened over break. Griffin didn't know what happened, and Willow couldn't see a reason for telling him. It would only worry him, and Willow would feel terrible if she ruined his day.

For a moment, Willow wondered if lying to him would hurt him even more. But, it wasn't really lying, only withholding the truth.

Satisfied with her decision, Willow completed her journey over to Griffin. He had his nose in a book as if he couldn't hear anyone else in the cafeteria. Willow sat down right next to him, an impish grin on her face.

"Griffin!" She greeted him cheerily. Willow cringed at the sickly sweet tone that entered her voice, but Griffin must not have heard it through the noise. He almost dropped his book, startled at the sudden interruption. When he realized who was speaking, a huge smile spread across his face.

"Salutations!" He replied. Willow shoved him over playfully on the bench.

Willow checked her watch, confused as to why so many people were already on campus. Well, she checked where her watch would've been.

"Griffin." He ignored her. "Griffin, what time is it? I left my watch at home." Griffin sighed dramatically and looked at her with his blue eyes.

"What do you mean, you left your watch at home? I see one right there, on your wrist." Griffin pointed to a bare spot of Willow's hand.

"It doesn't seem to be working well, you know. I think it must be broken." Willow contributed to the joke. "So... Can I see your watch?" Willow asked sheepishly. Griffin laughed and twisted his wrist so that she could see. 11:49. Turns out she had been a bit late, who'd have thought?!

"Thanks, Griffin. You're the best friend ever. And not just because you let me use your watch." Willow spoke mischievously.

He waved her off. "Yeah, whatever." Willow picked at her peanut butter and jelly sandwich for a moment before turning back to Griffin.

"Griffin," Willow started. "I have a proposition for you." Griffin knew better than to trust Willow when she addressed him like that, but curiosity would always be his downfall. Closing his book with his fingers between the pages, Griffin smiled sweetly at Willow.

"And what would that be?" Griffin interrogated her. Willow knew she had caught his attention, and spoke quickly before he could change his mind.

"Well, I was thinking that we could go to the school library and steal a few books?" Willow suggested. Griffin groaned, but the smile never left his face.

"Willow, that is a very irresponsible idea! We can't do that," he scolded.

"But Griffin, we'll return them! And besides, I know you want to come. You only have around ten pages left of that book that you're reading right now." Willow attempted to seem professional, but her childlike excitement seeped through.

"I could just *go* to the library for that, why should I accept your proposition?" Griffin matched Willow's official tone of voice while reasoning with her.

"It'll be fun…" Willow coaxed. *And it might be the last time I go to the Apollodorus Academy Library.*

"Right." Griffin sighed. "Let's get going then. We wouldn't want to go after the library closed." Griffin was willing to follow along with Willow. Each time he told himself he would only go to stop her if she decided to do something too impulsive or reckless. But Griffin also knew that Willow would never do something endangering. He trusted her. He also knew that he was going for the thrill of it. Griffin would never admit it, but he did in fact enjoy Willow's plots and schemes.

Willow stood up from the bench, leaving the peanut butter and jelly sandwich behind. Griffin slung his backpack over his shoulder, and walked beside her. Nobody would notice their absence in the crowds of a school cafeteria.

After they exited the company of other people, Griffin turned to Willow. "What's the plan? If you're dragging me into this then we better not get caught." Willow put her hands up the same way criminals do when the cops show up.

"Woah, woah, woah! I did not drag you into this, you agreed to come. And the plan is... well the plan is to get a book, and then leave. That's really all there is to it." Willow lowered her hands slowly and shrugged. By the time Willow was finished explaining the plan that did not exist, they had arrived at the doors of the library. The library did not look like a building of its time. Walking into it flooded the senses with the familiar smell of old books. The library was silent, much to the librarian's satisfaction. There were a few kids scattered around studying or reading, but none made a sound. It made it much harder to steal a book from

29

the library if the slightest sound would send all eyes your way. Instead of analyzing the situation and re-evaluating the lack of plan, Willow walked straight up to one of the aisles, took four books, and walked back quickly, straight past the wooden front desk with the librarian reading something on her computer, to where Griffin stood, gaping still by the door. Willow figured she really had nothing to lose anymore.

Willow walked straight out the door, Griffin following close behind. "Willow?! What was that?" Griffin was snapped out of his shock.

"The plan! Duh. Here, I got you the book you wanted." Willow stuck out a copy of *The Hobbit,* looking awfully smug. Griffin sighed as he took the book.

"You aren't invincible, you know? Librarians can be scary if they want to... But, thanks, Willow. You know you didn't do anything all that special, right? We basically just checked books out of the library?" Willow was beaming after the thank you, and Griffin worked hard to make the girl a bit more modest.

"Ah, but it was fun, Griffin! More fun is what you need in your life. That is what I am here for." Willow spoke in an announcer voice as she pointed to herself. "Now then... want to go to the forest?"

It wasn't a matter of want. It was tradition, and they both knew that. Griffin nodded his head, a response he didn't have to think about doing anymore.

"Great!" Willow replied the same way every time. The forest may be their special, favorite place that they went to all the time, but Willow didn't want a thing to change. Things would stay the same for as long as she could help it.

As they entered the woods, Griffin searched for a stick. It was an odd habit of his, yet another tradition. He found a stick that he was satisfied with before fiddling with it for the rest of the adventure.

"Oh! So I've been meaning to tell you about this dragon. Actually, you want to see him?" Willow became enthusiastic over the prospect. It was the only thought residing in her mind that was filled with pure bliss. The other "happy" thoughts were tainted with a bittersweet taste.

Gone was Griffin's shy shell as Willow remembered the story she had found about the dragons.

"Yeah! Show it to me." Griffin exclaimed. Willow leaned against a great oak tree. It's leaves shook down onto her hair and around her feet. Willow delved into her description, allowing Griffin and herself to imagine a world of their own. She didn't even have to close her eyes. By her first thought, they were transported into a medieval kingdom where a dragon lay with an egg. *It's leathery wings extended over the egg, offering it protection. The dragon let out a low guttural noise as the egg began quaking. Slivers of cracks began to appear on the pearly white shell, growing and growing until a little creature popped out. The older dragon's sounds of protection turned to coos of adornment, and the little dragon let out shouts of excitement.* Right as the dragon opened its wing for the first time, the image flickered out of view.

"What was that?" Griffin asked cautiously. "Why did you stop?" He approached Willow slowly. "Willow, what happened?" Willow stood there, unmoving.

"Sorry, it won't happen again." Willow ran out of the forest, not looking back at Griffin's protests. "Come find me at Mx. Wilde's!" she called back. She took pity on him as she ran to the English teacher's classroom. Mx. Wilde let students do work for other classes in their classroom so they could get inspiration. Willow did her work there as much as she could. Either there or the library. They both felt comfortable, and cozy, unlike her home.

Willow had known perfectly well why she stopped telling the story to Griffin. It was the flicker of doubt that crossed her mind. The thread of worry that had woven it's way into every creation of Willow's brain, wrapping her thoughts in its itchy warmth and long woolen scarves. It was more than that, though. The stories had always flown off her tongue, like a native language. Willow knew in the back of her mind that stories were what would keep her at Apollodorus Academy. She needed some answers, and she needed Mx. Wilde.

Willow ran through the school, her hair flowing behind her, her brown eyes focused ahead of her. The cliques huddled in groups were whispering. Hopefully about her. She thought it was interesting when people were talking about her behind her back. She wasn't mad, or annoyed. Just curious. Plus, she had to talk to Mx. Wilde before Griffin got there, and Griffin was fast. Just as fast as she was. She swerved to miss students, and she ignored the teachers telling her to slow down. She was a good kid, although most of the time she was lost in her imagination, the teachers liked her. She almost slipped on the newly cleaned hallway, before just barely regaining her balance.

A teacher from one of the older grades glared at her, and Willow suppressed a smile. The school was not the most relaxed, but they wouldn't get that mad at her for running. Willow had to tell Mx. Wilde about her imagination before it got out of hand. Right? What if it disappeared completely one day? What if her entire imagination just flickered out one day, forgotten? Then she and Griffin wouldn't be friends anymore, and they would eventually grow apart. It was an impossible possibility, Willow tried to convince herself. Griffin was her best friend in the whole world. Finn had a best friend once. He couldn't remember their name.

Willow smelled the aroma of dinner being prepared in the kitchen. She waved quickly to one of the lunch ladies. Willow waved to her every morning. The woman stood out with her dyed red hair that was wrapped into a bun that resembled an apple. She was different, just like Willow.

Running through the school, she imagined she was at Hogwarts. That the headmaster had a long, white beard, and was older than anyone thought. She always imagined that her science teacher was secretly Professor McGonagall. But today as she ran down the hall, all she saw was her relatively old, straight brown-haired, very strict, science teacher. Uh-oh.

"Willow! Nice to see you back at school. How was your break?" Ms. Wyatt, her science teacher, asked. Willow stopped short in front of her.

33

"Boring. Nothing exciting. Thanks for asking. I hope you had a good break. Glad to be back. Listen, I'd love to chat, but I have to go. I'll talk to you later." Willow said quickly. Without waiting for a response, Willow left her old fashioned teacher looking flustered.

"Mx. Wilde, I need to talk to you." Willow rushed into her English teacher's classroom before backing up to wait for Mx. Wilde's invitation into the room. She waited in the beautiful oak doorway.

"What's up?" Mx. Wilde, the best English teacher in the entire world, asked as they stopped grading papers to commit to paying attention to their student. That was one of Willow's favorite qualities about Mx. Wilde. Whenever you were talking to them, they made you feel like the most important person in the world. Willow was one of Mx. Wilde's favorite students, although they weren't supposed to have favorites. They also adored Griffin. Willow and Griffin were their best students, and had the largest imaginations they had ever seen. They loved talking to Willow and Griffin, about whatever was going on in the kids' lives, or even just about school work. They hoped that Willow and Griffin knew that they could go to them for whatever they needed.

"I just…" Willow paused. Could she really tell Mx. Wilde everything? Willow trusted them wholeheartedly, but she stopped trusting herself. Willow couldn't tell her yet. Not about the scholarship. Telling Mx. Wilde about the scholarship would only change things. Aside from the scholarship, Willow knew she needed to talk about the story, or lack thereof. She was just having an off day, right? That had to be it. So... since she was just having an off day, why did she have to tell her teacher, and get them involved, or worse. Worried? Willow was fine. She'd be better tomorrow. She just needed rest. Willow would tell both Mx. Wilde and Griffin by the end of the week. She promised herself, and decided not to tell Mx. Wilde yet. "I just had a question about the homework." Mx. Wilde nodded, curious.

Willow pulled her purple English binder out of her backpack. The cover of the binder was full of colorful little doodles that she and Griffin had drawn on it when they first met. "I wanted to know how many lines our poem has to be?" She asked. Mx. Wilde frowned. Usually Willow's questions were more creative. Less... ordinary and more about the feel, or thoughts the lines have. Not what a normal student would ask. Something so... Willow.

"Fourteen lines. Is that all?" Mx. Wilde asked. Willow nodded. What was wrong with her? Willow's cheeks burned. She couldn't come up with anything better? Nothing? She was about to say something else - maybe apologizing for such a bland question, even though she had nothing to apologize for - but Griffin ran into the room before she could make an even bigger fool of herself.

Chapter 4

Griffin was left alone, standing in the forest. There was nobody around him, nobody to hear his thoughts pound against his head. Autumn leaves drifted down around him, and birds cooed from atop the trees. The nature was peaceful. Quiet, as always, but something had changed, and he knew it. Nothing monumental had happened to signal the shift, but he knew that the events that just occurred would change things. For some reason, Willow had slipped up. She told the story wrong. It meant nothing to him, after all, it was just one moment. Evidently, Willow did not have the same thoughts.

Shocked out of his stunned stupor as a bird narrowly flew by his head, Griffin finally processed Willow's words. *"Come find me at Mx. Wilde's,"* she had said. Griffin sighed as he began the run to the other side of campus.

Willow always ran, she never hid. Games of hide and seek were treacherous— the girl never stayed in one spot for long. Griffin pumped his arms faster, not wanting Willow to disappear from the classroom before he arrived.

He ran past students, occasionally knocking into their sides. If he caused them to drop something, he'd stop to help, but if he just brushed across their arms, he'd shout a loud "sorry!" back to them. Usually he would stop to make sure they were okay, but he needed to get to Willow.

He whirred by the circle of cars that was dropping kids off, by the dining hall, by the library, by the math and science building, two of the three dorm buildings, and finally in front of the doors to the humanities building. That was where Mx. Wilde's classroom was, amongst other teachers. Griffin shoved his shoulder into the door with more force than he intended. Either that, or the doors were lighter than he remembered. The doors banged into the wall, and Griffin cringed. The door handle would probably imprint the wall, but he would fix that later. Griffin stumbled up the red and white tiled staircase. The echoey chamber made his footsteps louder than they should've been. He sort of liked the sounds— it made his shoes sound like drums.

At the top of the staircase, Griffin ran down the hall. He saw that Mx. Wilde's door was open, and saw Willow's familiar caramel colored hair leaning against the door.

"Hi, Mx. Wilde!" Griffin shouted down the hall. He was determined to get Willow to stay put. Mx. Wilde peeked their head of messy black hair out the door. Their hair was streaked with the familiar vibrant white lines that contrasted the dark hair. Technically you weren't allowed to have dyed hair at Apollodorus, but Mx. Wilde joked that the headmaster couldn't say anything about their hair because it would mean they were suggesting Mx. Wilde was old. Mx. Wilde chuckled, and they yelled back dramatically.

"Ah, yes. Mr. Rivers! Is there really a need to shout down the hall?" they joked. Griffin laughed. The English teacher always acted like they were more of a student, well... until it came to Shakespeare. Nothing came between Mx. Wilde and their *Julius Caesar* lessons. Griffin jogged up to the door and smirked.

"Probably not. Just saw the door open," he gestured to the door, or rather Willow. "Hey, Willow! What's up?" Griffin walked into the room, and sat on one of the swivel chairs.

Mumbling, Willow responded, "Nothing. You just saw me five minutes ago." Mx. Wilde frowned, and ushered Willow into the room, closing the door behind her. Mx. Wilde put the familiar grin back on their face. "What's up, guys!? It's been a long, but much needed, break." Mx. Wilde tried to break the tension. "Read any good books lately? A break from school doesn't mean a break from reading!" Griffin decided to go along with Mx. Wilde's contagious positivity and leave Willow a bit of time to think. After all, she wasn't going anywhere.

"No books worth mentioning. Though I did pull out a copy of *The Hobbit* from the library," Griffin shot a mischievous glance towards Willow, who shot him back a tentative grin. "I can't wait to read that."

Mx. Wilde shook their head and chuckled. "Only you two would spend break reading. I'm afraid your generation doesn't appreciate a good old fashioned book anymore." Willow frowned at Mx. Wilde's words. If an entire generation could 'grow out' of such a wonderful thing, how long would it be before she grew out of her 'childish, imaginative phase,' as Uncle David so kindly put it? Griffin spoke up, troubled by Mx. Wilde's words as well.

"We should make them appreciate books more," he said. Mx. Wilde chuckled.

"Griffin, I believe people have come up with that idea before. What do you think my whole job as your English teacher is? If you could find a way to bring back the art of reading, you, Mr. Griffin, would be a hero." Griffin smirked.

"Is that a challenge, Mx. Wilde?" Griffin was trying to put on a show for Willow to make her feel better, but he also took the conversation seriously. He would do anything to instill his love of books in others. Even if it meant 'stealing' from the school library.

"Oh, it certainly is!" Mx. Wilde checked their watch. "Oh, there's some staff meeting today. I've got to run. But you two can stay here if you want. I'll leave the windows open." Mx. Wilde cracked open the windows, and they raced out of the room. Griffin and Willow were left in an awkward silence.

"Just saying, I don't really want to talk about it." Willow squirmed uncomfortably, but spoke confidently. She had already made her decision to keep Griffin in the dark for now. Griffin sighed.

"I know, we don't have to. Not now, anyways." Griffin sat down on the radiator next to the window, and Willow came over next to him.

"Are you really going to take Mx. Wilde up on their challenge?" Willow asked. Griffin feigned a surprised look.

"Of course! What, you want in?" Griffin took on an impish grin. Willow nodded vigorously.

"Can't have you stealing any more books without me," Willow knocked into his shoulder playfully. Griffin held his hands up, like a suspect getting caught by the police.

"Woah, woah, woah, who said anything about stealing any books?"

"I did. Now are we going to get started, or just sit around all day doing nothing? We've got an hour til dinner. Plenty of time to start our rigorous journey!" Willow stood up in the middle of her speech, taking on a pose of a superhero. Griffin was exhausted from the events of the day, but he was just happy that Willow seemed back to "normal."

"I hate to break it to you, but the first step for our 'rigorous journey' is unpacking our bags." Willow groaned and flopped against the windows. "Come on," Griffin said playfully. Willow closed her eyes and started fake sleeping.

"Can't. I'm asleep," Willow said.

"You can't talk if you're asleep," Griffin grinned. Willow snapped up, and shot a joking glare towards Griffin. "Great. Let's go." Griffin pulled Willow up to a standing position. Willow turned serious for a moment.

"Thanks, Griffin." She was sincere, he could tell. He gave her a soft smile, different from the mischievous one that so often appeared on his face.

"Yeah, no problem. What're friends for? Now come on." Griffin dragged Willow out of Mx. Wilde's classroom, down the staircase, and out the door. Unfortunately, the two weren't on the same floor of the dorms. They tried to separate the girls and boys dorm rooms as much as they could. But they were in the same building because of the odd ratio of boys to girls. The two made their way over to their dorm building, Tolkien Dorm. It sat on the furthest end of the campus, bordering the edge of the school property lines. There was something special about the Tolkien Dorm. Something about the way it looked over the valley, the way you could see the sun rise on the river, the deer you could see mulling through the forest. The other dorms were fine, Shakespeare Dorm and Austen Dorm, but they were at the center of the campus. The buildings themselves were gorgeous, with their rustic wooden insides and their stone brick exterior. But if you looked outside the window, all you saw was more buildings.

The cobbled pathways had a thin stream of students walking to their dorms to unpack their belongings, but it wasn't nearly as crowded as it had been before. As Willow and Griffin got closer and closer to Tolkien Dorm, the students around them seemed to disappear. Unless you were in Tolkien Dorm, there was no real reason to be on the far side of campus. Griffin approached the dorm doors, and held it open for Willow to walk through. He followed in shortly behind her.

"Meet me at dinner. And before you ask, I think it's meatloaf tonight," Willow said as the two stood at the bottom of the staircase. Griffin made a face of disgust.

"Why is it always meatloaf after breaks? We just came back, why can't they serve something else?" Willow laughed at him, forgetting for a moment about unpacking.

"Oh, quit complaining! The salad bar is open, you know," Willow suggested.

"But that's too healthy," Griffin complained. Willow shook her head in amusement. "We can decide what I'll have for dinner later. I've got a lot of stuff to unpack, so I'll see you at dinner." Griffin waved to Willow as he walked backwards up the staircase, and disappeared at the top.

Willow was left standing at the bottom of the staircase. It was rare that she stopped to take in her surroundings. It was the rare occasion as Willow looked at what she could lose. She stopped and looked around, taking in the familiarity of the building. The rough wooden walls, the rows of doors, the soft rhythm of song playing down the hallway. Here, she was home. She didn't need dragons or fairies to make her feel like she belonged.

Willow made her way down the hallway and stopped in front of her door. Willow creaked open the door and stepped inside the room. The blinds covered the windows, which immediately caught Willow's attention. She promptly uncovered the windows, and the soft afternoon light peered into her room. Willow's bed still sat on the left side of the room, messily made. On the right was the perfectly made bed that had been collecting dust all year. Willow's dorm mate had switched schools right before the year began, so Willow had been left without a dorm mate. It was fine by her; more time to think, fewer people staring at her. Besides, Willow had heard rumors about bad roommates from Griffin's dorm mate, Tyler. Tyler was much more in tune with the other students. He could tell you practically anything about any of the students, and was basically the designated party planner for the entire grade.

Willow slowly started unloading the black suitcase with her belongings. She had left most of her clothes in the closet before they went on break, so her bags were fairly empty aside from books, drawing supplies, and trinkets that Willow had become oddly attached to. She set a little snow globe on the night table beside her bed. The globe contained an entire city, covered in a blanket of fresh snow. Willow liked to think that people might live there. She liked to think that maybe she could live there when she grew up. Not in a snow globe, of course. Just the city. With people strolling down the roads, kids building snowmen on the sidewalks, the music of traffic on the streets, and the soft snow that layered the buildings.

Willow mindlessly unpacked the rest of her things, and she tuned out the thoughts of the scholarship and her family. She was at Apollodorus Academy, and that was all that mattered. She placed her things back just the way they had been before she left. With the new addition of Willow's poetry homework, of course. She cringed, thinking about the question she had asked Mx. Wilde earlier. Willow would apologize to them later, she decided. By the time Willow had finished putting her belongings away, the sun shone dimmer into her room, covered by the cloak of night and a few early stars. Willow checked the time on her tiny clock. 6:53. Dinner was in seven minutes, she remembered. There was a campfire that night. It was an optional one, but Griffin and Willow had never passed up on an opportunity for extra s'mores and spooky stories.

Willow left her dorm, not wanting to be late to dinner, and joined into the crowd of people walking to dinner. It felt nice going to dinner with people other than her family, without the fear of the heavy chandelier over the dining table. When the group of kids entered the dining hall, it was exactly how it should be. A flood of students all in uniform who just wanted dinner. Willow shivered at the thought of only ever eating dinner with her family. She maneuvered through the chaos over to the bench where Griffin already sat, reading the copy of *The Hobbit* that the two had stolen from the library. Willow and Griffin always waited for the food lines to peeter out before standing up to get their food.

"Hello there," Willow greeted Griffin. He looked up from the book and grinned.

Griffin grabbed a slip of paper from his backpack, and he slid it into his book before rolling his eyes playfully. He had already made quite a dent in the number of pages left in the book. Willow figured he had probably finished cleaning his dorm room early, or Tyler had cleaned the whole room for him.

The line of hungry students began to decrease, and Willow and Griffin got up at the exact same time to get dinner trays. The other perk of coming on the line late were the dinner trays. The ones that had been washed first were on the bottom, and those trays were always the cleanest. Cleaning hundreds of trays was bound to get tiring, and it showed from the globs of food that stuck to the trays closer to the top of the stack. Griffin and Willow grabbed their *clean,* beige trays, and they split lines. Willow stayed on the regular line for meatloaf, but Griffin walked over to a small salad station.

The food at Apollodorus Academy was mediocre. Willow ate it happily compared to the burnt meals that graced the tables at her home in Wood Creek, but she wished it wasn't so bland. There were salt shakers scattered throughout the cafeteria, but it was difficult to locate one and even more difficult to locate one with any salt in it.

Willow and Griffin reunited after getting their dinners, and sat down on the bench where they had waited earlier. The bench didn't have a table attached, so the two had to eat with their food in their laps. That was probably why the bench was always empty, but Willow and Griffin took full advantage of the empty seat in the otherwise squished cafeteria seating.

"How's the meatloaf?" Griffin asked between bites of salad.

"Is good," Willow spoke through a mouthful of food. Griffin laughed.

"Remember, we still have the campfire tonight, so don't fill up on dining hall meatloaf," Griffin warned. Willow sometimes saw him as her voice of reason, but then there were times when she wasn't so sure, a prime example being the library 'robbery.'

"Let's set a goal for how many s'mores each of us can eat. I bet I can beat you," Willow challenged Griffin.

"I bet you can beat me too. But how about... five for me?"

"Only five?! Well I think I can have twelve," Willow declared confidently. If Willow was going to be forced to leave Apollodorus Academy, she would eat every s'more possible while she could. Though, the idea of Willow after twelve s'mores at 9:30 P.M was slightly terrifying. Her mind would most likely wander off into another world and set off an onslaught of fire-breathing dragons. Fire-breathing dragons were quite possibly the only thing that could compare to Willow after twelve s'mores.

"You might be able to handle twelve s'mores, but I'm not sure how the rest of us could handle twelve s'mores. And besides, we need you to still have brain capacity to brainstorm for Mx. Wilde's challenge!" Willow facepalmed.

"It's not like my brain is going to eat the marshmallows, Griffin." A very vivid image popped into Willow's head. *The prefrontal cortex had morphed into a marshmallow, along with the rest of the brain. The marshmallows mingled and melted, hopping around the brain. They had silly smiley faces printed across their fronts and little stick feet. A dragon swooped in suddenly, and let out a roar of fire. The marshmallow faces disappeared as the marshmallows flamed and blackened, the same way that they did over a campfire. With the demise of the marshmallows, the vivid image disappeared from Willow's mind.* Willow reminded herself to be cautious about burning her marshmallows later that night.

Students around them started putting their dishes up on the counter. Willow and Griffin shoveled food down their mouths, rushing to finish dinner on time to get to the campfire. As soon as their plates were cleared, they raced out of the dining hall, not wanting to be the last ones out.

There were only ten or twelve students around the campfire when Griffin and Willow arrived. The rest of the kids probably wanted a night in after break, or they still hadn't gotten back to school. Ms. Wyatt, their science teacher, was supervising the campfire that night. Willow felt a pang of guilt for leaving the conversation with Ms. Wyatt so abruptly earlier, but she brushed it aside as she picked up a fluffy marshmallow off of the table. Autumn leaves crunched under her hiking boots as she walked, and the smell of campfire was sent through the air.

"Griffin, are we still on for the marshmallow contest?!" Willow shouted to him. He was sitting by the fire, playing with twigs on the ground.

"Yeah, but I'll give you a head start!" He shouted back. Some of the other students looked at the two of them oddly, but they quickly resumed their chattering. Griffin pulled out his iPod and mini speaker from his backpack. "Do you guys mind if we turn on some music?" Griffin asked the rest of the kids. A chorus of "not at all!" and "sure, sounds good," sounded, and Griffin grinned. He scrolled down the list of songs, and found one he was satisfied with. *Click.* He pressed the button, and the familiar intro to "Mr. Blue Sky" turned on. Willow whipped around to turn towards the fire as soon as she heard the speaker softly releasing the music. Willow set the marshmallow carefully on the table, and walked over to the fire. The words started, and a large grin split onto Willow's face.

After many songs later, Willow finally sat down on one of the dusty tree stumps. She had tired herself out air guitaring and lip syncing. Griffin had joined in too, using one of the twigs with a marshmallow on top as a microphone and actually screaming the lyrics instead of lip synching. The music had been full of laughter. Willow kept pausing the songs every so often to try and hear Griffin singing. He really did have a wonderful voice. The few students that had been there were mostly gone, leaving only a few seniors behind. It was their last year at Apollodorus Academy, and they didn't want to miss a single moment. Willow was bitterly reminded that this could be her last year, too.

Willow's marshmallow still sat at the table, and the fire was getting low. The small licks of flame were surrounded by red embers and the remains of firewood. Ms. Wyatt still sat boredly by the table on her phone, waiting for the kids to decide it was time to go. They technically didn't have to leave for another hour or so. Ms. Wyatt was wonderfully lively during the day, but it seemed that as soon as the stars came out, the woman just wanted to go to bed. Willow turned to Griffin, and she whispered softly,

"Griffin, the fire." Sleepily, Griffin looked towards the fire.

"Hmm? What about it?" Willow laughed at how dazed he was. She spoke softly so that she didn't startle him out of his sleepiness.

"If you look at it closely, you can see a dragon." Griffin squinted from the log seats as Willow used her finger to outline its fiery body. "See? The wings and the tail?" Griffin nodded, a little bit more awake.

"Yeah... of course I see. Can a dragon made out of fire still breathe fire?" He seemed genuinely confused, so Willow put some thought into it.

"I think it could. Though really it's up to us, isn't it?" Willow asked with a chuckle. Griffin laughed back.

"Yeah, I guess it is." Griffin pointed to a smaller lick of flame that danced on the outskirts of the fire. "There's another one." He didn't trace it out like Willow had. He didn't need to. Willow could see it immediately. She could identify every curve and ridge on the dragon's body, and was relieved how quickly she realized it. Her earlier doubts floated away. Willow was the one that made the dragon come to life in a way that the other kids never could.

"We've got to name it." Griffin said abruptly. Willow stared at him.

"The fake dragon?" Griffin shook his head.

"No. All of... this!" He gestured to the dragons, Willow, and himself. Willow laughed confusedly.

"You mean the dragons, and the stories, and the world? Is that what you mean?" Griffin nodded vigorously.

"Yeah. Let's call it... um..." Griffin trailed off. "I don't know," Griffin said helplessly. The idea drifted away into the wind.

It seemed as if names were very important. Names made things so much more real, but so much less mysterious. An imagination without a name would either be forgotten and crumble, or would create a world with the deepest of mysteries.

The fire soon died out. As the flames crumbled so did the dragons, leaving only embers of their fiery breath. Ms. Wyatt had fallen asleep with her face on the phone, and she had rolled her head onto the side of the table. The seniors had finished all of the marshmallows, including the one that Willow had left sitting on the table. The s'mores contest had been forgotten, having been replaced by new memories by the campfire. Seeing that the fire had gone out, the two older kids left, leaving only Ms. Wyatt and the faltering embers for company. Willow and Griffin silently cleaned up all of the s'mores ingredients and doused the fire with water.

Ms. Wyatt began mumbling in her sleep, her mind on science. "The mitochondria is the powerhouse of the cell," she snored. Willow and Griffin remembered that they needed to break her slumber.

"It's your turn to wake her up," Willow whispered to Griffin.

"No, I distinctly remember I did it last time." Griffin tried to avert the duty. Willow laughed.

"No, I did it last time! Remember, she knocked all the graham crackers off of the table when I woke her up last time?" Griffin frowned and stroked a fake beard.

"Wasn't that two times ago?" Both of them burst out into laughter. Ms. Wyatt's eyes popped open, startled. Willow and Griffin tried to stifle their laughter as the science teacher blinked, incredibly confused.

"Willow? Griffin? Oh, what time is it? I must've fallen asleep." Always polite to teachers, Willow walked over to Ms. Wyatt.

"Don't worry, we've cleaned up the things. It's only 10:00. We were just heading in for the night." Ms. Wyatt nodded, though she wasn't really paying attention. She pat Willow on the shoulder.

"Good, good. Well then, I'd best be heading to sleep."
Ms. Wyatt walked back towards the center of campus, and
disappeared into the night. Willow and Griffin followed
closely behind, too tired to talk. The only sounds were
their feet crunching on the leaves and the birds singing
throughout the sky.

At the bottom of the dorm building they parted again.
Willow watched as Griffin trudged up the stairs, then turned
down the hallway and into her room. Willow quickly slid
her hiking boots off, and discarded her uniform on the
floor. She put on a pair of pajamas and pulled her dark
brown hair into a ponytail. Exhausted, she flopped into
the fluffy mattress and entered the realm of dreams.

Chapter 5

Willow awoke in a white void, she stood but somehow she felt no floor. She wiggled her arms and legs around, they were there. She was there. "Am I dead?" Willow whispered, but no sound came out of her mouth.

Instead she saw her words literally bounce across the floor, written in comic sans font and fade into the distance along with the sound of them hitting the surface of this void, or whatever the white blanket of nothingness that lay beneath her was. She stood there, shocked. "Griffin?" Her friend's name floated up into the pale, solid white sky like a balloon, it looked like some sort of 3d graffiti art in inflated typing. The words popped just before they were out of sight and somewhere in the possibly endless sky. Willow wondered why the words were different fonts, then a thought struck her. Maybe it was her mind giving emotion to the words.

"The Fallon family," she said. Her words appeared in front of her and fell to the floor with a thud. They were made of solid rock with a chain coming out from them, tied to her ankle. The words started to slip into the ground, dragging her down. She shrieked. No letters came out this time, and slowly, she started to go under.

Willow remembered a phrase suddenly. "Lucid dream." The words escaped her mouth and yet again the two words appeared just above her. They were in her own handwriting. They slowly started to float up into the sky. She grabbed the "u" before the "lucid dream" was out of reach.

Willow was pulled up from under the ground. The lucid dream's upward force was too much for her family. She felt safe, like maybe they couldn't burden her here. She felt the chain break and her leg slipped free from the floor. After she was free the word descended to her level. She wondered how she knew those words. She paced for a bit, searching her brain. The "lucid dream" followed her, always staying about a foot away from her. Suddenly she remembered and the "lucid dream" melted into a square where a memory was projected.

She remembered this, it was about two weeks ago. She had learned about it in Mx. Wilde's class. She had been sitting in the front of the class, her teacher's hand wrote intensively on the chalkboard. Soon, their voice came in over the sound of the class chatter.

"Earlier, we talked about subconscious and conscious." Mx. Wilde said as they pointed to the drawings of brains and diagrams on the chalkboard. "Now we have also covered dreams, why they exist, how our subconscious affects them, and why they are important. Now we will talk about a Lucid dream." They wrote "lucid dream" on the chalkboard in big letters.

Mx. Wilde strode over to the other side of the chalkboard. "A lucid dream is when you are conscious of having a dream during a dream, and sometimes you can even take control of your dream." They wrote down each point on the chalkboard. The point of view turned downwards in Willow's mind, and on Willow's loose leaf sheet of notes, she saw her hand write "lucid dream." The notes morphed into the same floating "lucid dream" that drifted through her mind like it had before.

Willow tried to corner herself in her mind. She tried to find a place in this place that was full of her dreams of mythical kingdoms and fantastical worlds. Wherever she turned, all she saw were the words of the plagued reality.

If this was really a lucid dream, she could choose what she sees, what this world was. She could turn this white void into the place she had lost.

"If I can control what happens next, then I want to go back! I want to go back to when I could see the wilderness and fight with dragons, I want to go back to a better place than this miserable world!" A few thoughts slid across her brain, stuck on the idea of going back. All she had ever wanted to do was conjure up her future, waiting to live it. Now that it had come, all she wanted to do was go back. Like all her other thoughts, this one slid off the surface of her brain like skates, bringing her words back to the center of attention.

As Willow spoke, her demands flowed out of her mouth, all black and random fonts. They clustered at the walls, piling up. She saw creeks and valleys through the cracks of the words, and she ran for them. Soon the word family appeared again, chained to her feet. This wasn't control, this was chaos.

Then more words that were chained to her appeared. The walls turned black and the rocky words and their chains became white. It wasn't right. Her mind was supposed to be her escape from the world.

Other words kept on coming, and soon, Willow was sucked into the floor.

Chapter 6

Willow woke up in a sweat, gasping for air. She pinched herself, reassuring herself it was just a dream, but she still couldn't get her heart to stop racing. She shut her eyes tight and opened them again. She pushed her covers aside, and got out of bed. She started pacing. Willow's pajamas were dark green, and her shirt and sweatpants had little dragons scattered on them. They had been a birthday present from Griffin the month earlier.

Willow slipped on her favorite slippers and opened the door before racing upstairs to find Griffin. She technically would have gotten in a lot of trouble for being out after curfew, but there weren't any teachers around. The hallway was eerily silent.

Instead of finding dragons playing, and other comforting things in the shadows around her, like usual, she saw scarier things, like the gunfire from a shadowy trench. Or her parents. Terrified, Willow sprinted faster to Griffin's room, only slipping once.

"Willow? It's one A.M! What's wrong?" Griffin asked, rubbing the exhausted look out of his eyes. He was wearing navy blue pajamas with pictures of Harry Potter characters drawn in cartoons. Griffin's hair was messed up in a Disney-style hairstyle that never seemed to go away when he brushed it in the morning. His roommate, Tyler, snored across the room.

Panting from her frantic run, Willow pulled Griffin out into the hallway so that they wouldn't wake Tyler.

"Griffin. I had a nightmare." Willow said. Griffin looked worried, but also confused. Whenever Willow had nightmares, she told Griffin about them the morning after. Not in the middle of the night, in dragon pajamas. "Not like, a stupid, immature nightmare. A real, vivid one. I would say words, right? And they would just... there was a-a memory? Of Mx. Wilde's class last week, when we learned about lucid dreams. In the dream, I was... I knew what was happening. Anyway, the words bounced off the floor, or popped. They had different fonts. Like... they expressed how I felt about these words." She explained.

"How was this a nightmare?" Griffin asked.

"I felt like I was drowning. I was sucked into the floor. It wasn't right, those words *weren't* supposed to be there." Willow admitted.

"Anything else you haven't told me? Because that seems like a really weird dream, and dreams are your subconscious." Griffin said. He thought Willow was going to say that there was nothing else. After all, they told each other everything. All of the good, bad, scary, comforting. Willow fidgeted nervously.

"Well... yeah. Griffin, I don't trust my mind anymore. My imagination is different now. It's spiraling out of control." Willow faltered. "My parents are also going to take me out of Apollodorus Academy if I don't get a scholarship." Willow confessed. Her shoulders felt lighter after telling her best friend, but she was also nervous about how he would react. It was a huge deal, but they would figure it out together. They always figured it out together.

After the lucid dream, she had to say something. She was too scared to ignore it.

"What?!?!" Griffin screamed. Willow shushed him.

"If teachers find out we are out after curfew..." Willow trailed off, and Griffin bit his lip. He knew she was right. But how could her imagination be *disappearing*? And why hadn't she told him that she might have to leave? Griffin thought she would tell him anything. He thought she *trusted* him. It wasn't his turn to feel hurt, though. He could only imagine what was going through Willow's mind. She shouldn't have to handle this all on her own.

"It'll be an adventure. You need this." Griffin declared. "Look. I've known you since we started at Apollodorus Academy. I know that this will make you feel better." Willow hesitated before nodding.

"Okay, good. Then about the scholarship. Willow, you should've told me." Willow held guilt in her eyes.

"I know, and I'm sorry. I really am, Griffin." Willow apologized.

"It's okay, Willow, honestly. I just wish you had told me," Griffin reassured her. "Now what?"

"Can we go tell Mx. Wilde?" Willow asked. She felt, well, kind of exhilarated from telling Griffin. She felt lighter.

"Umm. Like I said, Willow. It's 1 am." Griffin pointed out.

"They won't care!" Willow exclaimed. Griffin started to protest but followed her to the teacher's apartment when she ran towards it alone. They got there quickly -- it was only a couple minutes away. Knocking on their door, Griffin sighed in exhaustion and leaned against the wall.

"Griffin? Willow? What are you two doing here?" Mx. Wilde asked, confused but also still half asleep. Willow and Griffin took turns explaining what had happened to their teacher.

"Willow, is this what you were going to tell me today when you came to my classroom?" Mx. Wilde asked after hearing the whole story. Willow nodded meekly. "Well, I know an awful lot about the scholarships here, being a teacher and all. There are plenty of options, I think they have music ones, art ones, creative writing ones... you name it! Willow, I'm sure that whatever the lucid dream was isn't because you lost your imagination. I never mentioned it in class, but a lucid dream is a strong sign of creativity. Maybe it was a little bit chaotic, but that's never stopped you before! You have a brilliant mind, Willow. If you're still worried in a few days, you can come back. But for now, I think everyone should go back to sleep. I'm giving you both permission to skip first period tomorrow. I believe you have my class. It should give you time to calm down and sleep in. It's late. Okay?" Mx. Wilde asked. Griffin and Willow agreed, and went back to their rooms. Griffin fell asleep immediately, but Willow tossed and turned for a while, her mind racing a mile a minute.

What if her imagination was gone for good soon? What would she do? She wouldn't be able to get any of the scholarships that Mx. Wilde had listed. Her parents would be happy, but she would be miserable. It's not like her parents understood her at all. They were, well, older than most parents of the kids her age. The only reason she was any use to her parents was to raise her as another carbon copy of themselves. She had always felt like an outsider.

Willow moved onto the next question she had to answer about the near future. She always struggled with the future, the infinite abyss of time is just too big a concept for anyone to handle. People always say to live life to the fullest as if time ends with it. In reality, time moves with or without life, whether the movement of it has a meaning anymore. Willow started an internal debate, her voice representing the defendant, the victim, the judge, the jury and the plaintiff. She didn't know whether time moved without meaning. She didn't know if time moved without a witness. Her mental jury agreed with this but she brought up the point that time hasn't waited thus far to make things easier. The court broke into madness, yelling, screaming. She tried to shut down the conversation, but it was easier said than done. She squeezed her eyes shut and tried to think about her friends and reality. She brought herself back to reality, wiped off the beads of sweat that had formed on her forehead. Willow turned over in her bed.

Did Mx. Wilde even have a real plan? They had made it seem like they did, but maybe they were just trying to get Willow and Griffin to calm down. Something was wrong, and Willow knew it. She was afraid of the world she had created to escape from the one she lived in. Maybe it was written in the stars that her utopias were destined to crumble.

Chapter 7

Willow sat up in her bed, fully awake. She hadn't slept for the remainder of the night, and she hadn't tried. Instead, she had been busy planning. The scholarships were looking very far away. She couldn't get one, no matter what Mx. Wilde said. Willow was fine with all of her academics, but she wasn't impressive enough for a scholarship. It was her creativity and her imagination that had always made her stand out in the crowd. It was her creativity that caused her trouble, but it also brought her light. But now, the light that it carried more closely resembled a raging fire. It was untamed, destructive, yet beautiful somehow. Willow wanted it controlled, back to normal. She wanted the one constant in her life to come back. She could think of only one way to do that. Willow left her room, still in her pajamas. She raced up to Griffin, hoping that he was awake.

The sun was already coming up, causing Griffin to twist away in the bed across the room. He tried to bury his eyes into the pillow, but he couldn't escape the rising sun. Groggily, he woke up and rubbed his eyes. He was met by Willow standing at the doorway.

"Willow? What time is it?" He yawned, checking his wrist for a watch that wasn't there. He had left it across the room when Willow had come to him about her dream.

"Time to get up, sleepy head!" Willow exclaimed. She was giddy with excitement for her newly made plan. Griffin shot her a glare as he pulled himself up to standing on the wooden floors. "Don't shoot the messenger! It's time for breakfast." Willow got out of bed with too much energy for any one person to have at this ungodly hour of the morning.

"Since when are you a morning person?" Griffin stared in amazement as Willow ushered him out of the room and down the stairs.

"Since today. Now meet me in the dining hall as soon as possible. I've got something to tell you." Willow responded on the way down the stairs, stopping right at the bottom. Willow sprinted to her room excitedly, leaving Griffin in the hallway.

"Why can't you just tell me now?!" Griffin was greeted by silence. "Willow!" Griffin complained jokingly. Willow always had to be extra mysterious. He didn't mind; it brought a little bit of fun to his life. Griffin walked back up to his dorm to get ready for breakfast. Tyler would be awfully confused.

Willow was alone in her room, with only the ticking of the clock and the creaking of the floorboards above her. She got clothes out anxiously, putting on the school uniform. She discarded her dragon pajamas on the ground, not caring to put them neatly into the laundry basket. Willow got ready as quickly as possible, not trusting herself not to chicken out before she told Griffin her idea.

Willow arrived early at breakfast. The doors were still closed, and they weren't letting anyone in yet. The smells of waffles wafted out through the cracks in the door, making Willow's stomach growl. Pictures popped into her head of waffles doused in chocolate chips and maple syrup. They disappeared quickly, leaving Willow's stomach growling in suspense.

A line of people started to gather behind Willow. Every student was sleepy eyed and yawning on the quiet morning. Normally Willow was never first in line, but today her mind wasn't on food. Instead it was coming up with every possible way that Griffin could react. For some reason only the negative outcomes made themselves known to Willow.

Willow stood on her toes with the strong hiking boots she wore as support. She spotted Griffin's figure coming closer to the line.

"Griffin!" Willow shouted, and ran away from the first spot in the breakfast line. The students that had gathered behind her stared in shock as the second student in line gladly claimed the first spot.

"I saw you ten minutes ago, what...?" Griffin trailed off, still half-asleep. The breakfast doors swung open loudly, and Willow and Griffin followed the mob of students into the dining hall. "So what did you want to tell me?" Griffin spoke nonchalantly, and Willow began to wish she could sound the same. Instead, she anxiously started explaining.

"We're leaving." She was met with a blank

stare. "We have to go somewhere— do something! If we don't, then I won't be able to stay here. I came up with this idea last night. We leave, go to the city, or the woods, or whatever, and then we can find my imagination, and then come back, and I'll get the scholarship. We'll take waffles with us. We can figure it all out. What do you think?"

"How are you going to get the scholarship? Isn't skipping school going to make you less likely to get one?" Griffin was more awake, but also much more confused. Willow shook her head vehemently.

"I can't get one until we do this! Don't you see? Whatever...

creativity I had before. That's out of my control now. I need it back." Willow was beginning to get frustrated. She knew that Griffin hadn't done anything wrong. Willow was angry with herself.

"So, you want me to ditch school with you to what, *find* your imagination?" Griffin shot her an incredulous glance, but it was ignored by Willow.

"Yes! Exactly. We'll come back after, and I'll

get my scholarship. Everything will go back to normal. It will be perfect." Willow smiled contently as she walked towards the breakfast line.

"No, Willow! I get that you don't want things to change, really I do, but this will change everything. It will jeopardize both of our enrollments at this school! And this is the exact opposite of what will get you a scholarship!" Griffin pleaded with her. He had never been this upset with Willow. Then again, she had never done something as reckless as this.

"At some point, I needed to choose what matters to me, Griffin. The only things I can think of are you, Apollodorus Academy, and my imagination. There is *nothing* for me in the real world. Going there will remind me how much I need the things that matter!" Willow went through the much rehearsed speech in her head. She had spent much of the night figuring out how to pitch her idea to Griffin. Once Willow was satisfied with her pitch, she practiced it til it was flawless. Until Griffin would see why they needed to go.

"And what about Finn?" Griffin's voice was deathly quiet. Willow had not anticipated the question, and her back went rigid. "Does he not matter to you? Does the man who usually makes you cookies and drives you to school not matter to you? Because he lives in the real world, Willow! You can't just pick and choose what parts of reality you want to live because not all of them are exactly what you want. What if somehow you get stuck in your mind and you can't leave!" Griffin was breathing heavily by the end of his outburst. Willow hadn't expected any outcome similar to what she had just experienced. The shouting hadn't even been that loud because of the noisy cafeteria.

"That would never happen." Willow protested.

"Well that's what I would have thought yesterday too! But your imagination is fading, Willow. It probably won't happen, but we can't know, and I can't lose you!" Griffin stated, his heart racing from yelling. He was desperate to convince Willow not to go on this trip.

"I thought you would be excited to go on an adventure?" Willow asked, sounding smaller than she was.

"I am! I am. Of course I am," Griffin ran his hand through his hair. "It's for the wrong reasons, Willow. You need to take a step back, and look around at what you have. If you can't do that right now, then just look in front of you. I'm right here." Griffin was about to continue, but then realized that Willow would go either way. But with Griffin, she would be safer. Griffin paused for a second before he spoke his next words. "Fine. I'll come with you." Griffin agreed because he knew that Willow would've. No matter how crazy a situation Griffin found himself in, Willow would always be there. In fact, she had been there. The consequences of the adventure would amount to nothing because, without Willow, Griffin probably wouldn't have even gotten to where he was.

Willow's face lit up, but Griffin hadn't finished. "If, if, you do what I said, and look around. I think you'll find you have a lot more than what you think." Griffin finished the deal, wondering if he made the right choice.

"Thank you, Griffin! Thank you." Willow spoke sincerely. Griffin knew how much this meant to her. "Okay, now let's get waffles! We'll pack after breakfast." Willow declared, walking up to the waffle line.

"This morning?!" Griffin said incredulously. Willow nodded her head from in front of him. "Do you have *no* impulse control?" He said. Willow turned around, laughing.

"Griffin, since when do I have impulse control?" Griffin honestly tried to think of a time when she had actually thought out a decision. Other than the one she had just made. No scenarios came into his mind. It was strange to think that the only situation Willow had ever really thought through was the most reckless of them all.

"Never." Griffin groaned, setting off a laugh for Willow. He hesitated for a moment. "Willow, can we leave a note for Mx. Wilde? They need to know what happened." Willow nodded seriously. She had thought about Mx. Wilde the night before. Leaving a note seemed like the best solution. If they were already gone, Mx. Wilde couldn't get them back.

"Yeah. Yeah, we can. No specifics, though. Mx. Wilde can't come to find us." Willow pronounced each word carefully. Griffin chuckled nervously.

"Do we even know the specifics?" He questioned. Willow grinned, which was not necessarily what Griffin had expected. Her answer confused him even more.

"Nope! Absolutely no clue." Willow used tongs to take a waffle from the bin on the lunch display. Griffin sighed.

"I already agreed, and I'm not backing out, but you can't expect me to blindly follow you into the world!" Griffin grabbed his own waffle, then added a second when nobody was looking.

"See, that's exactly what we have to do! We've got to get away from plans and live spontaneously for once. You can't tell me that's not exciting?" Willow ripped a bite out of her waffle. She knew him too well.

"Right. Great." Griffin ran his fingers through his hair, letting out a breath. "I'm going to turn in my poetry assignment." Willow smirked at that. Even while planning to ditch school, Griffin still wanted to turn in a short poetry assignment. "And I'll slip the note in. After that, we can leave." Willow nodded in agreement, taking another bite out of the crispy waffle.

"Don't worry, Griffin!"

"I have no idea what you are talking about. I'm fine!" Griffin said, fidgeting with the waffle in his hands.

"You are worrying. It's gonna be great, I'm telling you! We'll come back, I'll get my scholarship, and then we can stay here. *Away* from the rest of the world." Willow seemed so excited that Griffin didn't have the heart to tell her that she would grow up and have to live in the real world. Or that she was diving headfirst in what she claimed to be the most terrible thing in the world: reality.

Griffin and Willow finished their waffles in silence. Griffin was too nervous to talk, and Willow was too excited. They walked briskly back to the Tolkien Dorm. It was a chilly morning complete with wind wiping around their faces, sending autumn leaves their way. The two parted to their separate rooms in silence, a mutual understanding between them. It may be their last time in their rooms for a while.

Willow walked into her room slowly, taking each step cautiously and carefully as if she didn't want to mess something up. She looked around, and a flood of worry entered her mind, washing away the excitement that she had felt that morning. What if it was the last time she ever had a home at Apollodorus Academy? What if she was sucked into the real world and got torn apart by the lies, wrongs, and order of real life? Would she be able to escape the grasps of society once she willingly entered their bonds? Willow packed the clothes she wanted to bring on her trip. It felt similar to when she had unpacked the day before, but this time the threat looming over her was different. She had created the threat for herself. If anything went wrong, it would be her fault.

Griffin trudged up the stairs. His footsteps made loud sounds as they smacked against the carpeted floors. His dorm door was left open, which meant that Tyler had just recently gone to breakfast. Tyler always woke up late. The breakfast doors waited for him to go through before closing each morning. Griffin walked through the door, closing it softly behind him with a click. Tyler had left his bed neatly folded, a contrast to the rest of the room. The walls were filled with papers that Tyler and Griffin had collected over the few years. Books were left half open, split at the spine on the floor. Griffin walked over to the wooden dresser. The top surface of it was covered in colored pencils and crayons.

Griffin opened one of the creaky drawers, the markers rolled around a little bit on the wood. He wasn't quite sure where to start. Was there a packing list for this kind of thing? Griffin started transferring clothes out from the drawers into his small suitcase. His favorite shirt, favorite pair of jeans, favorite beanie. Griffin quickly realized he didn't have much to bring with him. Most of his belongings were trinkets he had picked up here and there as reminders. They reminded him that there were things the world had to offer that he couldn't find at Apollodorus Academy. Coins from the pressed penny machines scattered around the country, snow globes, teddy bears with hats. Some were just moments. Moments where the water lapped at Griffin's toes on the beach, moments where Griffin saw families walking down the street hand in hand.

Griffin zipped up his suitcase, still half empty. He made his bed quickly, perhaps a first time experience. Griffin clutched his poetry homework and letter for Mx. Wilde in his hand as he rolled the suitcase out the door.

Willow was standing at the bottom of the staircase as Griffin's suitcase bumped down the stairs.

"You ready?" She asked. Griffin nodded firmly.

"Ready." Griffin sounded confident in his answer. Curious, he returned the question. "You ready?" Willow took a look around before responding.

"Ready."

Chapter 8

Griffin and Willow walked out of the
Tolkien Dorm, possibly for the last time. The pair
were headed to the language arts building. They both
were dragging small suitcases behind them, which would've
been a strange sight if it hadn't been a boarding school.
Many of the kids carried suitcases instead of backpacks. It
was easier since they already had suitcases for each trip to
school, and it motivated them to actually put away their
clothes. Once Griffin and Willow arrived at the building,
they waited outside the doors.

"Right. I'm going to Mx. Wilde's. Wait right
here. We've got to leave as soon as I come back: it's
seven. Mx. Wilde will be back soon with their coffee, so
be ready to leave." Griffin took a last look at his poetry
assignment. *The Road Not Taken.* Robert Frost. The note
on top of it was scrawled out in his messy handwriting:

Dear Mx. Wilde,
Willow and I will be out of school. We need
to take care of a few things. Please don't
worry, and don't come looking. We'll be back
soon :). We'll miss you!
  Griffin and Willow

It was short and to the point. Griffin gave
Willow a one-armed hug as he walked into the building.

His footsteps echoed down the halls. There was nobody
there to absorb the sound of his sneakers. Griffin knew that
he should've been quick to get out of the building, but he
found himself taking his time. He stared at the bulletin
boards with the school news, at the teacher's doors that
were covered in "Welcome!" decorations year-round.

Griffin stood in front of Mx. Wilde's door.

Tentatively, he placed his hand on the doorknob, the
cool metal contrasting against the warmth of his hand.
He twisted the knob, opening the door with ease. Mx.
Wilde left their door unlocked in the mornings, allowing
students to turn in projects last minute. Griffin hated to
take advantage of the privilege, but he slipped the note
and assignment into the pile anyways. With a last look
behind him, he left the room.

Griffin met back up with Willow outside the building. "Did you do it?" Willow asked, smiling. Griffin nodded
and shot a small smile back at her.

"Yep. I did it. Let's go!" Griffin grabbed his suitcase and
rolled it behind him. The leaves crunched as they entwined
themselves into the plastic wheels. Willow trailed closely
behind him, the path of leaves cleared by Griffin's suitcase.
"So where are we going?"

"This way." Willow pointed to the road that continued on past the Apollodorus Academy.

"I think there's a train station nearby. Did you bring money?" Willow came to a screeching halt. She had forgotten to ask Griffin to bring money. He nodded nonetheless as he pulled a few dollars out of his front pocket, then put them away. It wasn't much money, but Griffin wasn't about to tell Willow that. They had already left a note for Mx. Wilde. There was no going back now.

"Where are we going after the train station?" Griffin asked. He wasn't surprised when Willow gave him a vague answer.

"I dunno. Roads are like rivers, follow them and they've got to lead you somewhere." Griffin shrugged in response. It seemed like the logical decision, though nothing was really logical about what they were doing. Griffin's loyalty to Willow never wavered; she was his best friend. He may not agree with what she had decided to do, but he would stick by her side anyways. She couldn't get rid of him that easily.

Right as they exited Apollodorus Academy campus, Griffin picked up a twig. He twirled

it in his hands as he took a last look at the school, then ran off to catch up with Willow.

The train station wasn't as far away as Willow had thought. Griffin still looked exhausted from the shorter than anticipated walk. It was still early in the morning, so the journey had been fairly quiet other than Griffin's incessant "are we there yet?"

Once they had arrived at the station, the platform was flooded with people. Workers mingling with families, suitcases coexisting with backpacks. It seemed as if all the world had gotten together just to meet up at the train station that day. Griffin was shocked out of his sleepy stupor, while Willow was put into a trance of amazement.

"I thought that train stations were meant to be dirty?" Willow asked in awe. Griffin shook his head incredulously.

"Dirty is not the first word I would use to describe th-" Griffin was cut off by the train rolling in. The wheels screeched against the rails as the train came to a halting stop right in front of Willow and Griffin. The doors opened without a sound, whisking Willow and Griffin into the belly of the train.

"Where are you headed today?" A voice sounded. Willow looked up at a tall man.

"What?" She asked, confused. Griffin answered instead.

"How far will twenty dollars take us?" Griffin waited patiently as the man ruffled through a clipboard of papers.

"That'd be Ardsas Station for two. Just by Walt City." The man responded. Griffin ruffled through his coat pocket and pulled out a small bundle of cash.

"Here." He handed it to the tall man, who nodded in response.

"Alright then, here you are." He handed Willow and Griffin two neatly cut tickets. Griffin grabbed his, and Willow took hers tentatively out of the man's hand with a small nod before running to catch up with Griffin.

"What just happened?" Willow whispered to Griffin, trying not to attract any unwanted attention. The two sat down in empty seats right by a large window. Griffin leaned in closer, talking quietly.

"We just bought tickets so that we can ride this train. Soon, that guy we just bought the tickets from is going to come by and put holes in our tickets so that we can't use them again. Have you never been on a train before?" Griffin asked. Willow shook her head.

"We always drive in a car back at home. We never really go anywhere anyways." Willow stared forlornly out the window as the train doors closed, and they began to move. Griffin put a comforting hand on her shoulder. Together they watched through the window as the trees blurred together, creating a landscape of rainbow pastels.

"Hello, there. May I please see your tickets?" A woman asked politely. Griffin took Willow's ticket and his own and gave them to the ticket collector. Willow heard the small clicks as the hole puncher ate its way through the paper. She wanted so desperately to be able to imagine that with each click, a portal opened to another world. She wanted to be able to imagine that each click was a magnifying glass that she could see mythical creatures through. The only thing Willow could see was a ticket that wasn't quite whole.

"Thank you!" Griffin said, taking the tickets back. He gave Willow's back to her, and she carefully tucked it into her suitcase. He flopped back into his seat and leaned his head against the cool glass of the window. "When I was little, the ticket collectors would use the hole puncher to punch a smiley face into my ticket." Griffin smiled as he recalled the memory. Willow leaned her head against the window next to Griffin. The pastel rainbow through the window turned into complete darkness. "We're in a tunnel now," Griffin explained, noticing Willow's perplexed expression. She nodded as her face cleared of confusion.

"I think I like trains." Willow remarked. There was something about the train that made her feel like a little kid again. But trains were a part of the real world, Willow reminded herself. If they were an asset to reality then they were an obstacle to her. Reality held no imagination, it was simply real.

The darkness of the tunnel was replaced by the blurred outdoors. The train began to slow, and the wildlife began to separate itself from the blended painting until the train came to a stop. A loud "*ding!*" sounded overhead, followed by the booming voice declaring the stop:

"We have arrived at Ardsas Station. The doors will now open." Willow and Griffin hurriedly got up, still getting stuck behind the mob of people trying to exit.

Willow and Griffin exited the train station, and they were greeted by a small string of shops across the road. The mob of people who were in front of them scattered themselves throughout the shops.

"We could stay here?" Griffin suggested. Willow shook her head vehemently.

"If the school or my parents come looking for us they might look here. Let's go down that road." Willow pointed to a road along the side of the shops. It was enveloped in trees. Their leaves drooped into the gravel path. Griffin shrugged and started down the path with Willow.

The road was fairly flat, and nobody was driving down it. It had to lead somewhere, but there were probably much easier ways to get there than on foot. As they walked, the wheels of Griffin and Willow's suitcases grinded against the loose gravel on the sides of the road. It was very notice-able when Willow stopped in her tracks.

"Waffle break!" She shouted. Griffin set his bags down and cheerily made his way over to Willow. Willow unzipped her bag and pulled out two waffles. She handed one over to Griffin. They both walked off of the side of the road onto the grass and sat down. Griffin and Willow munched thoughtfully on their waffles.

"Tell me a story," Griffin spoke, his words garbled by a mouthful of waffle.

"Once upon a time there was a Lillow and a Criffin who sat on the side of a road eating waffles." Willow said as she stuffed another bite of waffle down her throat. Grif-fin laughed.

"Sounds like a great story." Griffin found it humor-ous, but he also knew that Willow never passed up on a chance to tell a story about imaginary adventures, king-doms, and dragons. Despite how much she hated reality, it seemed to Griffin that Willow was clutching onto it as a last resort.

"It is. And the Lillow and the Criffin just ran away from school to get back to school." Willow said.

"Well, it sounds crazy when you put it that way!" Grif-fin accused Willow. Griffin stood up and wiped his hands on his jeans. "When do you think we'll get into town?" Griffin checked his watch that he had picked up from the dorm room.

"Maybe an hour or two? I don't really know." Willow shrugged. Griffin groaned, *so* excited at the prospect of walking for two more hours.

"Oh, how did you ever drag me into this?" Griffin asked dramatically, falling into the pillowy grass behind him. Willow stood up, finished with her waffle. She stood over Griffin's body, sprawled out on the ground, and she put her hand out.

"Come on!" Willow laughed, amused by his dramatics. Griffin took her hand and pulled himself up off of the ground.

"Guess what I brought?" Griffin asked as he raised an eyebrow mischievously.

"I don't know. What?" Willow zipped up the suitcase and pulled it up onto its wheels. Griffin let out an exasperated sigh.

"You're supposed to guess." He reached into the front pocket of the suitcase. His hand came out with his iPod clutched in it.

"You're a lifesaver, Griffin! Put it on shuffle." Willow came over and watched as Griffin clicked the little buttons, turning the music on and the volume up. It didn't matter how loud the music was. Nobody was nearby to hear it. Griffin turned the volume all the way up and put the iPod into his jeans pocket.

"Now that we got the music, let's keep going." Griffin and Willow started down the road. It was either a great shame or a great fortune that nobody saw Griffin and Willow as they danced and skipped down the middle of the road.

Willow and Griffin gradually slowed as the day went on. The songs had repeated at least four times over. The two never got tired of the songs, but it had come to the point where they knew which was next even on the shuffle setting Griffin had his iPod on. The sun was getting lazy in the sky, drooping down as a blanket of reds, oranges, and pinks was pulled over it.

"We're almost there!" Willow encouraged Griffin. "I think." She muttered under her breath, not loud enough for Griffin to hear. They were both getting tired. Griffin and Willow rounded the corner of the turn, their bags dragging lazily behind them. As they came around the corner, a big green sign greeted them.

WALT CITY
"WHERE DREAMS COME TRUE!"
1 MILE

Griffin wasn't looking up, but Willow saw the sign immediately.

"Griffin, how fast can you run a mile?" She grinned.

"Hmm?" Griffin looked up, confused as to what Willow was asking. Willow could tell the

moment he saw the sign. "Oh. Oh! Eight minutes." Willow smirked.

"I bet I can go faster." She took off running without waiting for Griffin.

"That's no fair! You get a head start, and you aren't as tired!" Griffin whined.

"I'll give you a five second head start," Willow bartered, stopping a little ways down the

road. Griffin figured it was about as good as he'd get and took off running.

Willow quickly got ahead of Griffin. The ground blurred under her, a sea of murky grey

water. She forgot about the rest of the world, focusing on the sound of her feet as they splashed in the sea of gravel. Willow could still hear Griffin's heavy breathing further behind her. Taking pity, she stopped running to wait for Griffin to catch up. It was only when she stopped running that she realized how heavy she was breathing. Willow bent over with her hands on her knees, catching her breath with closed eyes. She heard Griffin's footsteps slow as he approached her.

"Willow." He said breathlessly. "Willow!" She slowly stood back up. "Look."

They were at the entrance of the city. Skyscrapers poked through the threads of the orange sky, and car horns blared throughout the streets. Willow was in awe of the beauty of it, until she remembered where she was. She was in a city, where people were hungry on the streets, where people worked all day becoming utterly consumed with money. How could something be so beautiful while holding the terrors of reality?

"Wow." Griffin stared starry-eyed at the city. Willow stayed silent. She'd decide her feelings about the city after she got her imagination back in control. After she got back to Apollodorus Academy.

"Where do we start?" Willow was overwhelmed by the options that presented themselves to her. The streets forked off into different directions, the buildings stretched down for miles and miles. It was all theirs to take and explore.

"There!" Griffin pointed to a small plot of land where a four person band was playing. There was a crowd gathered around the musicians, cheering and dancing. He dragged Willow over. The music got louder and clearer as the two crossed roads carefully to get closer. They got closer and closer until they were part of the crowd, narrowly avoiding feet. It was difficult to maneuver two suitcases through, but Willow and Griffin managed. Willow saw a band she didn't recognize playing on the corner, and a few people dropping dollars into his hat that sat in front of him. They'd never heard the music that was being played before -- it wasn't on Griffin's playlist. Willow and Griffin danced to it nonetheless.

It seemed as if no time had gone by at all when the band thanked the crowd for listening and began to pack up. The crowd thinned out, going back to wherever they lived in the maze called Walt City. Willow and Griffin lingered around for a while before heading off. The sky was dark, covered in constellations. Covered in stories. Aiding the stars were the street signs that illuminated the city. It could never be entirely shrouded in darkness no matter how hard the cloak of night tried to throw itself over the city.

"Where are we going to sleep, Willow?" Griffin asked. A dozen other realizations rushed to his mind, but his sleepy mind put sleep in the front.

"We could go back out of the city just for the night. I'm worried about staying here, there are so many people." Willow hadn't really gotten to this part of planning. Each small detail of her plan had been perfected to a t. It was intricately webbed into her brain. Somehow, she had missed the details associated with reality. Griffin nodded along sleepily.

"Okay." He began walking sluggishly out of the city, Willow close behind. The energy that they had while dancing to the music drained out of them like the light of the sky. Willow and Griffin settled where the buildings had thinned out, skyscrapers morphing into barren trees of a lonely park. Their leaves had all fallen and created a crackling, fiery colored blanket across the ground. The park had been abandoned as the night sky flushed all the people into the still-colorful city. The silence was slightly haunting, and the whispers of the breeze made themselves heard. Griffin and Willow covered the ground with their own blankets they had brought from Apollodorus Academy, and they lied down. Griffin fell asleep immediately, exhausted from the chaos of the day. Willow found herself staring at the sky. She had always seen the stars as constellations. They were united. They had stories, tragedies, happy endings. But now when she looked at the stars, all she saw were the stars themselves. Twinkling softly, entrancing her with their beauty. They no longer were associated with stories. Instead, the complex stories were replaced with a wonderful simplicity.

Willow drifted off to sleep, and for the first time that she could remember, the land of dreams was empty. No splashes of paint, dragons, or kingdoms. Just a blank slate that waited patiently for Willow to paint her dreams on its canvas.

Chapter 9

The morning light shed through the trees, asking Willow and Griffin to wake up. Willow sat up sleepily, her title as a morning person disappearing after only one day. Leaves were entwined in her thick brown hair. Willow flipped over to face Griffin, who was lying flat on his back a few feet away.

"Griffin, are you awake?" Willow asked. Some birds and squirrels rushed out of the trees at the sudden noise. A small blue jay landed at her feet as she took in the scene. Griffin groaned as he flopped over.

"Unfortunately, yes." Griffin took his beanie off and cleaned the leaves off of it. "Where to, captain?" Griffin watched as Willow ruffled through her bag.

"Breakfast. Waffle?" Willow offered Griffin a cold waffle. He took the waffle and unhappily picked at it, pulling off all the ridges and popping them in his mouth.

"We're going to run out of waffles at some point. We'll need other food soon, Willow." Griffin pointed out. Willow frowned, ripping a large bite out of her waffle. Crumbs from where it ripped scattered on the grass, attracting little finches down to the ground. "Guessing you didn't bring any money?" Griffin asked. He had used his money on the train tickets. Willow shook her head.

"I didn't have any. I'm not allowed to bring money to Apollodorus Academy. In case I use it for something scandalous." Willow joked around while she played with leaves on the ground, not making eye contact. Griffin shot her a small smile before returning to the issue at hand.

"Right, sorry. We need money. Any ideas?" Griffin began to think of ways to get money, hoping that Willow would pitch in. After a few moments of thinking, Willow sighed.

"I got nothing. You?" Willow looked hopefully towards Griffin. He knew he couldn't say nothing. Both of them needed this. An inkling of an idea popped into his head.

"We could play music! On the streets, like the band we saw yesterday. I can sing and play guitar. We don't have a guitar, though. I could just sing." Griffin began to ramble. "And you can sing too! I've got my song notebook, I can sing songs from that." Griffin paused excitedly as the idea formed. "Wait, do you think we need a permit? If we don't explicitly ask for money we probably don't. Even if they tell us we need one, we'll just say we didn't know." He looked to Willow for approval. She was grinning widely.

"You're a genius, Griffin!" Willow stood up immediately. "Let's go."

"Right now? We just barely got up!" Griffin laughed as Willow dragged him off of the ground. She was eager to listen to Griffin play music for other people. *You're eager to go out into the real world?* Willow's mind asked her, confused. Willow waved off her thoughts.

"Yes, right now! Come on." Willow pulled their bags and Griffin behind her.

"I'm feeling a strong sense of de já vu." Griffin said, still being dragged.

"If you were more cooperative I wouldn't have to drag you as much!" Willow said innocently, batting her eyelashes. Griffin chuckled, wriggling himself out of Willow's grip.

"Okay, okay, I'm coming!" Griffin put his hands up like a criminal caught by a cop at the scene of the robbery. Willow and Griffin ran back into the city border, stopping at the first road. The city had already woken up, and cars were racing across the roads. Willow nearly ran into traffic multiple times, but Griffin put his hand in front of her each time. They skipped across crosswalks, only stepping on the white lines when they could. The trip across the city was full of laughs until the two of them arrived at the empty lot.

"Are you going to sing?" Griffin asked Willow.

"I don't think I can. I can't think of any songs." Willow always sang her own songs. They were beautifully crafted in the mines of her mind, instantly molded into delightful tunes that got stuck in everyone's head for days. Willow didn't trust herself to sing anymore. The hammers that shaped the songs swung wildly around her head, serving no purpose other than chaos.

"You can always sing one of mine." Griffin offered kindly. Willow politely declined.

"No, thanks. Those are your songs. They're brilliant, but they're yours. Besides, maybe listening to you will help me get back to normal." Willow shrugged nonchalantly. The thrill of running through the city streets had worn off. Griffin moved on skeptically.

"Okay. Do I just start singing?" Griffin asked nervously. Sometimes Willow forgot that this was a new experience for him too. He always knew what to do. Willow nodded her head, trying to look sure of herself.

"Uh huh. Just start singing. Like how you do it when it's just me." Willow knew it was easier said than done, but she felt completely useless if she couldn't give Griffin confidence. Griffin nodded, taking a deep breath before he began to sing.

Griffin started off softly. He recited the words from his original songs effortlessly, but his words weren't heard. People walked past, unhearing. The most that anyone stopped for was to try to figure out if they heard a faint voice and where it was coming from. Most of those people decided that they were hearing things and continued on their way.

"Hey, Griffin? Maybe sing a bit louder?" Willow suggested once he had finished the song. She spoke in a softer tone, not fitting her usual hyper demeanor. Willow knew that Griffin was very brave for singing in a large city, and she didn't want to discourage him from continuing. Griffin nodded in agreement, starting the next song.

When he opened his mouth, his voice sounded loudly around the block. To be heard over the city cacophony was a difficult task, but Griffin managed. People began to stop by, some left money, some listened, some waited til the end of the song for conversation. The more people that stopped by, the more Griffin's confidence grew. The more people that stopped by, the more Willow felt like she was sinking into the crowd. Griffin didn't need her anymore, she was just another fan.

Willow sat down on a small rock right next to Griffin. Griffin's singing went into her right ear while the sounds of the city entered her left ear. They didn't mix. It wasn't right. It had to be one or the other. Willow uncomfortably listened as the sounds clashed against each other in her mind, watching the people pass by. They treaded along the walkways in their polished black shoes and fancy dark slacks. They carried briefcases in their watch adorned hands.

Willow tried to imagine herself as one of the grown ups. The same monotonous schedules every day. She couldn't imagine herself being so consumed by work, though she supposed it wasn't too different from her imagination. *That can't be right,* Willow thought to herself. Imagination and work were two very different things. Imagination was bright, colorful, and brilliant. Work seemed like an anchor, tearing people down. *Isn't that what your imagination is doing to you?* The voice sounded again in her head.

Griffin's voice cut off as he finished another song. Willow was surprised to see that the crowd in front of him was still standing there, clapping. Griffin smiled so naturally in front of them. It was Willow's one chance to go on an adventure. An adventure that would thrill and challenge her. She had simply passed it up. Battling imaginary dragons and going on quests like knights was fun, but Willow knew how to do it. She realized bitterly that she had fallen into her own monotonous schedule. Willow had gone and grown up.

Chapter 10

Willow sat, perched next to Griffin, for a few more songs, lost in thought before sprinting through the crowd of people. She knew it was selfish. She knew Griffin deserved more than that after his hard work. She knew he shouldn't have been the one chasing after her. She knew so many things, and yet it seemed she knew nothing.

"Willow! Wait! Where are you going?" Griffin ran after her with the small sum of money he had managed to acquire. He was held back only by the barricades of traffic. The metal demons with their roaring horns and tire feet. Willow's figure got smaller as it retreated into the distance, and Griffin's hard-earned crowd began to disperse, confused at what had happened to their entertainment.

Finally, the traffic came to somewhat of a stop, and Griffin managed to make his way across the road. He sprinted down the sidewalks, trying his best to follow Willow through the sea of people. Her figure came back into view, causing Griffin to sprint even faster. There wasn't much use in being tied for the fastest person in school when you were chasing the person you were tied with. Griffin watched as Willow rounded the corner into a park. Griffin slowed his pace once he realized she was stopping at a bench.

"Willow? What's wrong?" Griffin asked after stopping in front of her. He was panting and out of breath, but somehow Willow was breathing normally.

"We need to leave," she said urgently. Griffin's protest got caught in his throat. He swallowed it down, determined to hear what she had to say. "This city is wonderful, but it's going to bring more harm than good. It was a risk before, but now it's a risk with no rewards. There's nothing for us here." Griffin thought back to his singing. It had been a wonderful time for him. There was something for him here- an entire future! He reminded himself that the journey wasn't about him. It was about Willow. As much as he wanted and envisioned that future for himself, he knew that wasn't the reason why he had come to Walt City. Willow would have done the same thing for him.

Griffin's parents loved him to no end, but they had no idea who he was. They took the time to love him, but not to get to know him. He was able to be himself around them, a thing that Willow couldn't do with her family. Griffin's parents didn't know about the encounters with bullies that he had at school. It was all well and good to be tied for the fastest kid in school, but the title seemed to have no use if Griffin didn't apply it to a sport with a ball. The only thing it seemed useful for was running away from the kids who did play sports. Griffin preferred spending time with Willow, who somehow managed to avoid all the criticism he had received. Maybe it was the way that she could make a conversation out of nothing at all that put her on good terms with everyone, maybe it was her endless babble that scared them away. Whatever it was struck Griffin as unique. The only people who would truly approach Willow as a friend were real. Whether or not she knew about the sorting system she had put up, Willow had let Griffin through. He got to know her, and it turned out she was one of the most *real* friends he had ever met. It was ironic because since the beginning of their friendship Willow had established her hatred for the *real* world.

Willow stuck by his side, her trust in him never wavering. They helped each other. Willow pretended the bullies were battalions of knights sent from otherworldly kingdoms. Griffin and Willow fought them off side by side. He wasn't going to give up on her now. Even if they did get kicked out of Apollodorus Academy, even if his entire life came crashing down, maybe Griffin's parents would finally pay attention to what was *actually* going on in his life instead of the utopia they created for him.

"Where do you want to go?" He asked. Willow looked up at him, her eyes helpless. She had nowhere to go. Griffin thought it over in his head. The school was sure to come looking for them soon. They had to leave anyway, and he was willing to take risks. "Let's take the subway?" Griffin asked. Willow grinned up at him. "The money we got from singing can pay for the tickets, and we'll still have extra!" Griffin felt a strange pull of possessiveness over the money, even though he knew they planned on using it anyways. After all, it had been his suggestion to use it. Willow nodded in agreement.

Griffin sighed. "Yeah, okay. Let's go." He was getting worn out from jumping place to place. There were no ties for him anywhere except for Willow. His tie to Willow seemed to be dragging him from train to train. Being dragged around seemed a small price to pay for the smile that only grew wider on Willow's face. Griffin made sure Willow was right behind him as they arrived at the aboveground entrance into the subway.

The two fourteen year olds walked down the stairs into the depths of the subway. They didn't touch the railings out of fear of what might be on them. The two of them dodged people walking in opposite directions. Nobody looked down at them, and nobody even noticed they were there. It was every person for themselves. Strangely, Willow felt satisfaction at the sight. It was how she imagined reality. A dirty place filled with ignorant people.

They were fish swimming against the currents, with no destination. The people surrounding them might be mindless, lifeless people, but at least they knew where they were going. At least they had a purpose.

Griffin grabbed Willow by the shoulders. "Hey, it's okay. We'll figure out something. We always do!" Willow didn't like the way Griffin said that, it sounded like he was reassuring himself more than anything.

"Griffin, I need you to tell me the truth." Willow said. Griffin heard the urgent tone in her voice, and his eyes shone with sincerity as he turned to look at Willow. "Do you think I will be able to get my imagination, or creativity, or whatever back?" Griffin had not been expecting that. Sure, it was the whole reason that they had left Apollodorus Academy, but Griffin had never thought it was a question of "if" rather than "when." If he was being honest with himself, he had never really looked at the possibility that this was all for nothing. He hadn't considered that maybe this was beyond their control, that maybe it was all just a part of getting older. He hadn't considered that maybe they were fighting time, waiting until it ran out. Walking on a tightrope pulled taught over a chasm, thinning until their own weight made it come crashing down. When everything came crashing down, it would be their fault.

Willow had asked for the truth, but Griffin couldn't bear to give it to her.

"Yeah. I do." Griffin said. Willow didn't look appeased by the answer. It had been exactly what she wanted to hear, but it wasn't any comfort.

They walked in silence to a bench and sat down, there was tension in the air. Willow and Griffin both knew that they had nowhere to go. "Let's search through our bags." Griffin suggested, "Maybe we'll find something to help us." Willow agreed reluctantly and swung her bag off her back and onto the bench. She opened her bag and rummaged through the various junk she had collected over their trip. She felt a piece of paper under her favourite Percy Jackson book, *The Sea of Monsters*. She pulled it out and saw a number on it. The paper had crumpled under the weight of the book but it was still readable. It read:

HELLO WILLOW, IT'S FINN HERE. I KNOW YOU'VE BEEN
HAVING SOME TROUBLE WITH YOUR FAMILY SO I
THOUGHT I'D SLIP THIS NUMBER INTO YOUR BAG INCASE
YOU EVER NEED IT   555 418 0092

I HOPE YOU'LL NEVER NEED THIS BUT IF YOU DO IT'S
HERE,

FROM, FINN
P.S IT'S MY NUMBER

Willow had never seen this before, it must have snuck its way in between the pages of her book. She could imagine living with Finn, to be fair. He had been much more caring than her family, much more accepting even though she only saw him for a little bit at the end of breaks. He was clumsy and didn't have the most dad-like job. She didn't think he even had any kids! Or at least any that she knew of. She had never thought about Finn much even though he was one of the people she couldn't bear life without. He cared about her, she was stunned. Her mind started swirling with different emotions, tears formed in her eyes.

"Willow!' Griffin exclaimed. "Are you okay?" Willow sniffled and stuffed all her welling emotions back down into her chest.

"Yeah, I think I know someone we could call." Hope rose in her chest as she easily found someone with a phone in the crowded underground. Willow had thought the hard part would be finding someone who was willing to lend her their phone, but that task seemed nearly as easy as the first.

Amidst the chaos of emotions, Griffin's bag was taken from its perch next to him. He hadn't noticed until it was gone. A volcano of eruptions burst inside of him. Griffin couldn't fathom why they lived in a world where people had to be cruel to one another instead of asking for help. His bag had been taken in a blink of an eye, before he even had a chance to do something about it. It made him wonder if Willow's imagination was already gone. But, it wasn't the time to be pessimistic.

Willow called Finn up, and he couldn't have sounded more eager to help. He said that he would be there in an hour since he had been getting fresh meat from a market a few towns over. Finn had no worries about any repercussions, all he cared about was Willow.

Willow realized how hungry she was after she hung up, Griffin felt just as starved. They could both hear each other's stomach grumbling, but all their money had been stolen when Griffin's bag had been taken. It was a good thing that Finn was going to come. If Griffin spent another day singing on the streets only to have his only reminder of hope stolen from him, he wasn't sure how long it would take for his facade to crack. He was still trying to stay optimistic, but he was getting to a breaking point. Willow couldn't blame him. It was painful to watch as the hardships he faced crack through his happy smile. There was only so much someone could take.

"So," Griffin questioned. "Are we telling Finn about everything that's happening?"

Willow sighed. She had been thinking for the past ten minutes about what they could do. Nothing came up.

She was stranded on an island without her imagination or any flares to call for help. Willow had drained the ocean of it's water. There was nothing left to do. "I think we're done with the imagination thing. I mean, hey! It happens, things come and go and I had a pretty good run." She said. "We've gone through hell for this, and nothing changed, Griffin. Nothing. Has. Changed. It was never meant to be," she said. Willow had been trying to tell herself this but she just couldn't. It was too much of a weight on her heart. She had to say it out loud to make it real. Willow wasn't going to keep chasing leads that didn't exist. As much as it hurt her to give up, continuing whatever quest she had started would only hurt Griffin.

Griffin stood in silence, gaping at Willow. "What did you just say?" He said slowly.

"We should stop the search, we should go back to school and our own lives, let's not look for something that can't be found," Willow said. She needed him to agree. Willow was doing it for him, and she had spent long enough convincing herself it was the right thing to do.

Griffin exploded.

"We are not stopping now. I have gone through all of this for you, understand?! I ran from home! Willow, I took on *fights* for you. I took on the world to try to get something that's *yours* back! Now you back out?! Willow, I just lost *everything* I was ever proud of making, just now! You don't get to say that while we are in the middle of losing everything and you're leaving me to do so by myself!"

Willow was shocked, but she was also angry. "Griffin, you're dreaming! Dreaming hasn't gotten us anywhere as we've seen!" The two had gathered an audience now, the people were looking at the show in the subway. They were staring in awe and wonder. Someone was chanting "Fight, Fight!" in the background. "You can't find something that's not real, Griffin!! If you can't touch it, if you can't see it. How do you find it!?" Willow yelled. She was tired, dirty and not in the mood to be fighting. Especially not her only friend, her only tether to her previous morals.

"Willow, imagination is not just your life. It's *my* life too. Have you ever taken the time to see that this isn't all about you!" Griffin screamed.

Willow felt flustered. She gave up on this for him and now he was calling her selfish?

"I never said that! I never said any of that! You're letting this crazy world twist your head! This place is bad, heartless and I don't know why in the world you'd want to keep on staying here! Griffin, I'm going to stop and I don't know about you but this is reality! It doesn't look like I can imagine anything here without getting hurt, so I'm going to go back to the repetitiveness of my family because at least I'm not losing everything there. Do you really want to become this? I don't, but it looks like destiny!" Willow yelled back.

This is what time asks of people, to conform to their society. To die without happiness. Time ends things on a bad note. Never on a dragon, never with a friend. Willow had been thrown out of the world of imagination, and she had been shunned from society. *Had society shunned her out, or had she shunned out society?* She belonged nowhere. She was only 14 ,but she knew time would catch up to her faster than she could run. "Time consumes all," was once one of her favourite quotes but she never understood the reality of it, the admiration of that black, misunderstood void had become a fear.

They stood in the circle of people, sweat forming on their faces. The pent up anger had all been let out. There was nothing left to say. They both stood apart, in silence. Some people had started filming them, others were leaving because the drama had stopped. Soon the crowd disappeared and they were forgotten. The bustle of the subway absorbed them, leaving them as a memory for the citizens. A little break from the ongoing loop of work and this dull grey life.

Willow and Griffin sat awkwardly down back next to each other. They were stuck together until Finn could take them their separate ways.

Willow's thoughts were consumed by anger. Her mind was a fiery battlefield, where there was nothing being imagined other than right and wrong. It was fire fighting fire, merging together until you couldn't tell which side was which.

Griffin wasn't one to hold grudges. He couldn't say the same for Willow as somehow she managed to hold a grudge on the entire world for a crime it never committed. She tricked herself into thinking the world had wronged her, creating a reality for herself where she could never be happy. *She* was the one who had envisioned the world as a terrible place. *She* was the one who decided she needed her imagination to escape from this "dreadful" world. Possibly, the most impressive thing she had conjured up was the extent of terrors in the real world.

An hour later, a big jeep pulled up. Willow was still not talking to Griffin, sitting in silence, but she motioned for him to follow her to Finn's car.

Willow popped open the door to the front seat of the car, letting Griffin sit in the back seats by himself. She was met by a concerned looking Finn.

"Willow? Are you alright?" Finn asked. Willow didn't want to say what she was thinking. That no, she wasn't alright. That she was watching her worlds come crashing together. That she was watching worlds that didn't belong together form alliances to take her down. She was everyone's common enemy. Instead, she nodded. Finn smiled a small, comforting smile, and looked to the back seat where Griffin was seated.

"You must be Griffin," Finn said cheerily. "I've heard lots about you." Griffin grinned at him, his troubles melting at the warmth of Finn's voice.

"And I, you! Willow talks about you quite a bit." Griffin said, making Finn break out into a broad grin. Willow sat guiltily in the front seat. She knew that Griffin was lying. Willow barely mentioned Finn. Of course, she regretted it now, but even as he aided her through thick and thin he was still just another part of reality for her to turn away. Finn turned back to face the wheel. "I reckon we better get back to my place! From what I hear, you two have been through quite the adventure." Finn started up the car again. Willow was uncharacteristically quiet. Her foot tapped against the floor of the car.

The long car ride was painfully awkward. Willow and Griffin were not talking, and Finn was too afraid to ask why. From what he had heard, they were best friends. Finn worried if he had read the situation wrong. Maybe the two of them were upset with him? Had he not come quick enough? Finn rolled down the car windows a crack so that the brisk autumn air was let in. It was the time of year between autumn and winter where the trees were bare with no leaves left to play in, but it wasn't yet cold enough for snow. It was the long, drawn out period of nothingness when weather teetered along the edges of the seasons.

Willow stared outside the car window, greeted by the same view, yet it looked so different to her. Instead of the emptiness that Finn saw, Willow saw the end. The end of autumn, her hopes, her imagination, her friendship with Griffin. While Finn knew that despite the desolate sight it would soon cascade into a winter wonderland, Willow saw no future for the winter. She only saw the end.

Chapter 11

After a long and painfully quiet car ride,

Willow, Griffin, and Finn arrived back into the town of Wood Creek. As they had been driving, Willow got more and more anxious about the plan to stay with Finn. She hadn't considered that it might get him into trouble with Apollodorus Academy and her parents. It put her in an even more sour mood once they had arrived.

Griffin felt so *tired*. He was more tired than he had been while walking to the city or while singing in the city. It was a different sort of tired that he had never quite felt before, since he always had Willow around. But now, she was dangling off of the tightrope, and she wouldn't let Griffin pull her up before she fell into the abyss. He couldn't come any closer, or she would fall, so instead he had to watch from afar as Willow teetered on the edge of gone.

Griffin found himself in front of a quaint store that he assumed was Finn's when the car stopped. He looked around quickly and found the town to be quite nice. It was difficult to see what Willow despised about it, but Griffin knew she disliked her family more than the town itself. If Willow took a step back and looked at the town, Griffin had a feeling she would fall in love with it. Wood Creek looked like it had popped into reality from a medieval fantasy town. The cobbled roads, the mingling people, the quaint shops. It was practically perfect.

Finn scratched the back of his head nervously.

"Alright then, I s'pose we should have something for dinner. I could cook up a few steaks, if you'd like?" Finn asked.

"Oh, I'm actually a vegetarian." Griffin said, looking down at his feet. Try telling a butcher you don't eat meat to their face.

"Oh! That's alright. Would you like to go to the bakery next door?" Finn offered. "Ms. Rosen makes delicious croissants." Finn often went to the bakery to talk with Ms. Rosen. She was a nice lady who knew her food. Finn had been fascinated by the art of breadmaking, something he had never been able to do very well.

"That sounds delicious, thank you!" Griffin glanced over towards Willow. Finn seemed to be waiting for her approval before taking them over to Ms. Rosen's bakery.

"Willow? How's a Ms. Rosen croissant sound?" Finn asked hesitantly. Willow finally looked up and nodded her approval.

"Never had it. If you like it, then it must be good!" Willow said, injecting a fake enthusiasm into her voice. Finn eyed her with concern, but didn't mention anything as he led her over to Ms. Rosen's.

The trio walked through the door, causing a little wind chime to signal their entry.

"I'll be with you in just a moment!" A far-away voice sounded. Willow assumed it was Ms. Rosen. Her voice sounded thin, but it held a level of happiness that Willow had always strived to achieve. That happiness was looking very far away.

Ms. Rosen rounded the corner. Her gray hair was knotted neatly into a bun, and her face was streaked with flour. Her blue flannel and black apron were covered in so much flour that the dark colors were turned light.

"Oh, hello! Finn I see you brought some folks with you?" Ms. Rosen wiped her hands on the apron, trying to clean them off, but it only covered them with more flour. Her eyes shone through the cloud of flour, seeming to be set on Finn.

"I'm Griffin, and that's Willow." Griffin introduced them both cheerily. It was hard not to be cheery around Ms. Rosen's floury appearance. Willow waved an introduction.

"How wonderful! Well I expect you didn't drop in just to say hi, though that would be nice. What could I get for you today?" Ms. Rosen asked Finn. He placed one hand on Griffin's shoulder and the other on Willow's.

"These two have worked up quite the appetite! I think they'd be very appreciative of a few croissants." Ms. Rosen smiled at the request.

"Perfect! I have some fresh ones that just came out of the oven only moments ago." She began to turn away to get the croissants when Finn interrupted.

"Jane, wait." Finn said, amused as he held out a little wad of cash. "Jane," or Ms. Rosen, turned around and let out a small chuckle. Finn shook his head affectionately.

"Ah, I'm always forgetting to ask these days." Ms. Rosen paused. "These are on the house. A first croissant from me is a magical experience! I can't afford to have it tarnished. If I could give out every croissant free, I would!" Ms. Rosen turned to retrieve the croissants. Finn was smiling broadly.

"Who's excited?!" Finn asked. He sounded like a little kid. Griffin and Willow didn't want to disappoint him with their answers. Of course they were excited, but a more fitting term would be very, very hungry. Willow didn't think his smile could get any larger, but when she spoke, it was as if his smile stretched the length of the world.

"I can't wait!" It was a genuine answer. Willow barely recognized her voice: somehow it had turned giddy with excitement. Griffin burst into a grin.

Griffin knew it had only been three words, but it seemed as if Willow had returned. It wasn't even a fraction of the excitement she had held in everyday life, but it was something. Griffin responded for Finn's benefit.

"I bet they're going to be awesome! Thanks for taking us here, Finn!" Finn smiled proudly. He finally felt like he had done something right.

Ms. Rosen came back out with her pair of patterned oven mitts and two croissants. Willow noticed the similarity between Finn's pair of oven mitts and Ms. Rosen's pair.

It had most likely been a gift from one of them. Everyone always seemed to be giving in the town of Wood Creek. Willow wondered when the well of giving would run dry.

Ms. Rosen dropped off the croissants, and nobody was disappointed.

"So, how are they?" Ms. Rosen asked eagerly. She had discarded her apron and put down her hair. She looked so much younger with the twinkle in her eyes. They were bright blue, like the ocean itself. It's water sparkled under the sun's glare, and it was full of playful splashing.

"They're great!" Griffin exclaimed. Willow nodded in agreement.

"I told you they were the best croissants," Finn said, winking up at the baker. Ms. Rosen smiled gratefully towards him. Willow and Griffin had already finished their croissants. "Well then, I guess we'd better get going. Thank you, Jane." Finn always sounded so sincere.

"Of course! Anytime." Jane responded, beginning to clean up the floury countertop. Griffin and Willow walked out the same door they entered with a quick thank you.

The three walked back towards Finn's shop in silence. It felt empty without the clatter of Ms. Rosen's bakery.

"Er, I suppose you must be too tired to talk. Why don't you head on back to the spare room in the back?" Finn said as he turned the keys to open the door. The big, old-fashioned clock that was stationed in the back of Finn's shop showed that it was only 5:00 P.M, but Willow and Griffin didn't argue as they headed back to the beds.

Willow felt terrible for not talking to Finn. She couldn't be more thankful for his hospitality, but she worried that her words would backfire on her. She worried that her words would be twisted and spoiled to aid the evils of the world. She hadn't meant to drive Griffin away with her words. But he hadn't really driven her away, had he? She was the one who tried to abandon their whole mission.

"Griffin, I'm sorry." Willow apologized as she sat on one of the twin beds. Griffin smiled to himself.

"I know." He responded. Anyone else would've said "it's okay," but Griffin knew Willow well enough that he knew it wasn't what she needed to hear. Willow needed to hear that Griffin truly understood she was sincere. That he understood her apology wasn't a playful joke. Her apology wasn't from another fantastical world.

That night as they went to sleep, the usual roles were reversed, and Griffin found himself staring at the ceiling while Willow passed out immediately. He had a sinking feeling, but it blended together with the rise of hope. He wasn't sure which to heed.

And, filled with the battle of hope and despair (and something in between), Griffin fell asleep.

Chapter 12

Griffin and Willow woke up the next morning to the loud sound of a crash outside the guest room. They shared a mutual look of confusion before popping out of their beds, still wearing the same clothes as the day before.

"Finn?" Willow said, holding the door open for Griffin to walk through. When she got no response, Willow called out again. "Finn?" Griffin rubbed his eyes tiredly.

"He probably just stepped outside for a bit."

Griffin mumbled, too tired to raise his voice to a normal level.

As if on cue, Finn walked back inside, beelining straight over to the right side of his shop.

It seemed as if he didn't see Willow and Griffin at all.

"Erm, Finn?" Willow said. Finn stumbled around, confused at who had called his name until he caught sight of

Willow and Griffin. A goofy smile planted itself on his face, and Finn switched directions over to Willow and Griffin.

"Just the two kids that I wanted to see!" Finn said brightly. Too brightly, if you asked Griffin. It was too early to have Finn's amount of energy. "Come on, I've got something to show you!" Finn led them over to a small stairway up into his attic. It was full of cobwebs and thick with dust, yet somehow in it's lack of use, it woke Griffin up. To him, it was a mysterious cavern just waiting to be explored. He would give up sleep for an adventure.

Willow stared at the creaky stairs in front of her. Any other week she would've jumped at the chance to climb them. But this week, Willow's mind filled with caution. *What if the stairs break, and you fall? What if there are rats up in the attic?* Any other week her only caution would've been a fantastical evil beast whose lair was in the attic. Rats and broken floorboards seemed much more scary and much more *real*.

Willow felt obligated to follow behind Griffin and Finn as they stepped up the stairs with ease.

Once they had reached the top of the stairs, without falling through much to Willow's relief, Finn flicked on a dim bulb. It shed a light on the contents of the attic, and Willow was pleased to see no rats anywhere. Instead, she saw boxes. Everything was in boxes, neatly lined up around the attic.

Willow tried to think of it like her mind.

One of the boxes in her mind contained imagination. Whether she had let it out, or boxed it in was the question.

Willow crouched over a dusty box. Finn was carrying two more over to her. He dropped them next to her, sending a wave of dust over the room.

"Sorry," he said sheepishly. Finn's attic was a treasure trove, there were at least fifty boxes along with 10 tied up stacks of papers. Finn wiped the sweat from his forehead.

"Well, this is my attic! It's full of everything you'd need for a history report, if you ever were doing a history report." He said cheerfully. Griffin was looking around the room in awe, glued to one spot.

"No kidding," Willow murmured in amazement. Finn's family history went way back. There were heirlooms from the 1800's, dated by the layers of dust. A grandfather clock stood tall in the corner. The bell had rusted over, and there was no way it could chime anymore. It's age must have gotten to it. Willow was worried that age would get to her as well, she used to feel like she had all the time in the world but now she never had enough. The days had started to turn into minutes, the time she had opened her eyes this morning had rapidly changed to her crouching in this attic with Finn, practically searching through time. She shook the thoughts out of her head. She knew time was the problem. It had to be.

"You okay?" Finn asked. His hand was on her shoulder. His care was always reassuring. He would always be there, and it brought her out of her anxious thoughts.

"Yeah, just got some shivers," Willow replied, and she wasn't lying. Thoughts like those always felt cold and heartless.

"Well, let's get searching then! We haven't got all-- well we do kind of have all day, but that's besides the point." Finn said. Willow laughed. Finn was the last person you'd expect to be awkward with his neighborly lifestyle, always lending help to others. He was very clumsy, though considering his size, it can't be easy doing day to day activities. Finn was the perfect example of a bull in a china shop.

The three of them started to go through the piles of papers and boxes, there was plenty of memorabilia that Willow would never know the meaning of. A purple bow, a ragged stuffed bear, letters upon letters that had a lifetime of story behind them. "You see this?" Finn asked, holding up a sketchbook with falling papers in front of him. "This was my sketchbook, I was never much of an artist but I always loved to draw."

"Can I see?" Willow asked curiously. She wondered how Finn's life was as a kid, but she knew asking might be rude. It would be just one more story left untold.

Reality crashed down on Willow. 7 billion people all had stories, hardships, lives that could change another's if someone heard their story. She shook the thoughts away, she had one goal at the moment, and that was getting her imagination back.

"Sure!" Finn said, cutting off her chain of negative thoughts. Finn opened up the sketchbook, but inside weren't the sketches she was expecting. On the first pages she saw faces that seemed to meld into the page made of hundreds of lines. It was almost abstract, but not quite. Nor was it realism. Willow couldn't place her finger on the style, but she wasn't exactly comforted by it. She did find some sort of calm in the madness of the art, it was unsettling.

"Woah," Willow said. Finn started to flip through the book. Every image had some hidden meaning, every line seeming liminal.

Finn then flipped to a page with some unicorns and flowers on it. Finn was a very interesting person. He let out a laugh. "I sure was a changeable kid." He sighed, closing the book with a soft clap. "Well, this is definitely a keeper." He picked the sketchbook to admire it one last time, and he went out to put it in his room.

Willow wondered if that's what she'd do when she grew up. Would she look back fondly on her memories with Griffin, and then file them away with the rest of her life? It hadn't occurred to her that after she graduated, she might move on. Griffin and her lost imagination would be just another faint memory, hidden among layers of dust.

Willow kept on looking through boxes and papers. She found an envelope with a picture falling out. The photograph had what looked like a young girl with a bit of acne on her forehead. She had a big smile on her face and dark brown eyes. She wrapped her arms around a tall redhead kid, and he had closed posture with some sort of band shirt, though she couldn't tell what band. He had a zit on his forehead. The photo was a polaroid, and it had a couple of lighter blotches. She picked up the letter, it was addressed to no one and seemed to be weathered with time. Carefully, she opened the letter, it read.

· Hey Finn,
I feel like it's been a thousand years since we've talked, and honestly, It could've been. Things are nowhere near as fun without you, school has sucked, and I know Winfried isn't the best place, but it has always seemed amazing when we explored it together. I haven't seen you since last summer, you never told me you were leaving school, and I have searched everywhere for your address, where are you? How have you been? I really miss seeing your drawings, your smile. Dammit Finn, I miss you. Please respond soon.

Love,

Autumn

P.s I got a dog! I know you always wanted one, and I was so excited to show you him, his name is going to be Betsy or Bennifer (whichever one you chose)

Just as she finished reading, Finn walked back into the room. He looked over to her and asked, "Hmm, what's that?"

"Oh, uh it's a letter from someone named Autumn." Willow answered.

Finn stood still, "I know that name." He said, searching his brain.

"Well, there's a photo as well," Willow said, she handed over the letter.

"Oh. Autumn. I forgot about this." Finn said. He saw the picture of the girl, and he smiled before his face slowly turning into a frown. Griffin walked over to see the letter. He had been wiping the dust off of the boxes. The memories seemed too delicate to touch, but too important to be veiled in the clouds of dust.

"Who is she?" Willow asked softly.

"Just a friend. A very old friend. From my past." Finn grabbed the letter and photo and walked to the other side of the attic. Willow and Griffin shared a glance. Griffin shrugged, and watched as Willow kept looking through Finn's stuff, although both of their minds were on Finn's letter from Autumn.

Griffin had barely caught a glance at the letter, but the words *"where are you?"* floated like a phantom across his mind. Would he spend the rest of his life chasing after Willow, wondering where she was? Would he chase Willow until his memory of her was no more than a shadow? Griffin needed Willow to, just this once, let him help her. If Willow rounded the corner away from Griffin while he wasn't looking, Griffin would spend the rest of his life wondering where she had gone.

Willow continued looking through the box that had contained Autumn's letter. Nothing else seemed to have as much significance as the tattered old letter. Willow peeked at the bottom, and she saw the white and black print of a newspaper. She pulled it out, and she ruffled through it's pages. The pages flapped in the air, letting out clouds of dust.

The paper was still intact, with it's black and white photos and strict font. Willow flipped to the second page, and she saw movies listed for showtimes that week. She recognized some of them from family movie nights. They always watched old movies if they watched anything at all.

Willow flipped through story after story, headline after headline. She found herself engrossed in the newspaper as if it were a fantasy novel. But it wasn't fantasy.

Everything that was written had happened. Every story that was meticulously typed out hadn't appeared on the page out of magic. There were happy stories, sad stories, stories Willow would have rather she hadn't seen. As much as Willow wanted to push reality away, she wanted to read its stories.

Willow thought about her own story. She had thought the blank page of her mind would've filled up immediately with words, but nothing appeared. Did she have no story? Had she done *nothing* with her life? If she disappeared on that very day, would she become another forgotten memory in a pile of papers?

But, wasn't that what she wanted? To fade away from reality?

Griffin was right, Willow couldn't pick and choose which parts of reality she wanted to live. Griffin was reality. Finn was reality. Apollodorus Academy was reality.

It was time to say goodbye to all of those things.

Chapter 13

Willow sat in the same spot, unmoving. Even though her mind had come crashing down, the world around her was still standing, and time was still ticking away. Willow hadn't realized that the newspaper had crinkled into her hand, forming a small paper ball. She tossed it quickly to the side, hoping that nobody would notice.

Griffin was looking at the old, dust covered books, oblivious to Willow's too-still figure. He remembered how he had told Mx. Wilde that he wanted more people to love reading. It seemed as if his mission had been lost. It was just another river that drifted into the ocean. All the troubles blended together until you couldn't quite see where one started or another ended.

"Can we go have breakfast? I'm getting hungry." Willow fibbed. She had lost all the appetite that she woke up with.

Until she got her imagination back, until she got to dine with sorcerers and witches, nothing would seem quite appetizing to her. All she wanted was an excuse to get out of the attic.

Finn was easily fooled. "I was hoping you'd ask that!" he exclaimed. Finn lumbered over to the attic entrance, Willow following close behind. Griffin reluctantly left the books behind, hoping to ask Finn about them later. Griffin actually had quite a few things to ask Finn. Willow had only ever referred to him as a kind butcher, a character in her story. But Griffin had seen his history and his memories, and Finn had a whole other story that Griffin guessed Willow knew nothing about. "Right this way." Finn ushered Griffin through the exit.

They had reached the bottom of the stairs when Griffin caught sight of the display on the table. He had sworn that the myriad of food hadn't been there when he had woken up that morning. What was once a splintering wooden table had been transformed into a feast that was fit for kings and queens. It wasn't enough for Willow, though. She was grateful for the food, of course. It was wonderful. But she wasn't going to fall into the same trap that she recalled from her history lessons. She remembered how Persephone had eaten the food from the Underworld, and then she had to stay there. Willow would eat the food that Finn made reluctantly, but she hoped with everything in her heart that it wouldn't bind her to reality.

"Finn, this is incredible!" Griffin said. Willow nodded in an echo.

"I got Jane— er... Ms. Rosen to help out! She was so excited when I asked for all this food. Oh, and Griffin I got you a muffin! I didn't know what kind you'd like, so I bought a few." Finn began to ramble. Griffin stared at him speechlessly. What had they done to deserve all that Finn had given them?

"Thank you. Really, Finn." Griffin said sincerely. Griffin looked over to Willow expectantly.

She seemed to notice as she responded with a quiet, "Thank you." Willow and Griffin walked over to the table and sat down. Finn stayed standing.

"Well let me know how it is!" Finn said excitedly, extracting a laugh out of Griffin. He twisted around in his chair so that he was facing Finn. Griffin held a chocolate muffin in his hand.

"Have a muffin, Finn." Griffin handed him the chocolate muffin, much to Finn's delight. Griffin was bitterly reminded of Willow's lost excitement. Her contagious excitement over the little things. S'mores, waffles, stealing from the school library. The memories all wandered in his mind.

Willow picked at the food in front of her. She was watching the interaction between Finn and Griffin resentfully. She overanalyzed their every word, trying to find anything to make it easier to leave them. She twisted their innocent words into weapons that were all aimed to fire at her.

"I'm going to step outside for a minute." Willow stood up abruptly and walked out of the room, immediately killing the light in the room.

Griffin and Finn shared a look once she was gone. They both remembered the Willow from before this whole mess. It had seemed as if she was regaining some of her excitement, getting some of the old Willow back, but then all the progress had flushed down the drain. Finn and Griffin searched their minds for something that they might've said, *anything* that would've upset Willow.

Griffin felt a small bubble of resentment pop up in his body. He tried to push it away, but he couldn't. It wasn't fair that he was throwing his life away for Willow, and in return, she was constantly trying to throw him away. It wasn't fair that Willow kept running, and she always expected Griffin to be there. One day, she'd turn around, and he wouldn't be there. She would push him away so many times that one time, he wouldn't come back.

Willow felt the cool air against her hair. It was easier to think outside. She knew what she had to do, but she couldn't bring herself to do it. She knew she had to leave Finn and Griffin. If Willow kept dragging Griffin along on her seemingly meaningless search for imagination, she would only be a burden on him. She would be selfish. Her only goal ever was to share her world with someone who loved it as much as she did. With Griffin. *But you've been selfish. You keep wanting for things that you can't have. When will you ever be satisfied?* A voice sounded in the back of her mind. Strangely, it sounded like her own. It wasn't her parents scolding her, or Griffin pleading with her, or Finn mentoring her. She was looking in a mirror, but the image wasn't how she had pictured it. *There's a difference between what you imagine is real, and what is real.*

Somehow, in a way that Willow couldn't fathom, Griffin was able to balance the worlds of reality and his imagination. They co-existed and made music, art, adventure, and stories. Willow had once been able to do that. *What went wrong?*

Willow turned back to face Finn's shop. Leaving something was so much harder once you were staring it right in the face. It was so much harder when you saw it vanish right in front of you.

Willow hadn't realized how silent it was outside until the opening of Finn's door shattered her thoughts. Now that she was thinking about it, it was much quieter than usual. Maybe everyone was still gone for Thanksgiving.

"Willow! We were just about to go on a walk. Wanna come?" Finn asked, a smile bright across his face. Willow planted an overly cheery smile on her face, seizing the opportunities that ran through her head.

"Yeah, I'll be right out in a minute! Let me just grab something from inside." Willow gave a thumbs up as she walked back into the store. Finn kept walking on ahead, slowly so that Willow could catch up once she came back out.

Griffin felt something strange in the exchange. As much as he wanted to believe Willow had regained her whole personality from just stepping outside, he knew the obstacles she was facing well enough.

Willow ran inside the shop. She had so little time. There wasn't enough time to get her suitcase, or any of her things. The only thing she had time to do was take money from Finn's cash register.

In one swoop of her hand, she had taken $100. One hundred dollars of Finn's carefully saved up money. One hundred dollars of the money that was left after he had bought them a feast for breakfast. One hundred dollars of the money that was left after Finn paid for the gas to drive them home. One hundred dollars of the money that was left after Finn bought ingredients to bake Willow cookies. One hundred dollars.

How could slips of paper be so important?

Willow vanished from the shop, leaving her suitcase with the golden train ticket in it behind.

Chapter 14

Griffin was the one that heard Finn's heavy shop door slammed shut that time. Finn carried on, unhearing, but Griffin whipped around. Willow was running in the opposite direction. Without him. Careful not to alert Finn, Griffin tried to keep his voice steady.

"Uh, Finn, I actually forgot something too.

I'll be right back." Griffin had already turned to run the other way. Finn nodded in response, not really paying attention. He was crouched over a lone flower growing in the sidewalk. It had probably been stepped on and biked over. It was probably far from its original color. But, it was still beautiful.

Griffin ran faster than he ever had. His strides were wild and long. His feet slapped against the sidewalk, squashing the flowers that grew along the way. Willow wouldn't outrun him this time. It seemed as if everything was a race now. He couldn't lose.

So, he ran.

He gained speed quickly. Griffin knew this was the fastest he had ever gone. The wind sent ripples through his light brown hair. He wondered if this was the speed of a train, flying down the tracks. Griffin felt free. He was being brought down and anchored to a million problems, but he felt more free than ever. That was the difference between him and Willow. He knew how to let go.

Willow's feet clutched onto the ground. She was slowed down by the things she was bound to and the things she couldn't bear to give away. Willow heard Griffin's steps approaching. This was exactly what she hadn't wanted. Willow wanted him to *stop*. She couldn't burden him anymore. She couldn't drag him down to whatever corner of her mind she was stuck in. *If she was burdening him, why did his steps sound so close?*

And then, he was right next to her. They were running side by side. Griffin's eyes flickered over to Willow's, but they never met. Willow's eyes were set ahead of her, on the sidewalk in front of her. Willow's eyes were set looking at the future, but not seeing the present. Griffin spotted determination in her eyes. Determination to run to a future that would never arrive.

Willow was running to get something,

Griffin was running to keep what he had.

"Willow, stop." Griffin said, almost at a whisper. She still looked straight ahead as she ran, unfazed.

"Willow, stop." Griffin said more forcefully. Willow didn't show any signs of hearing
Griffin.

"Willow, what about Finn?!" Griffin spoke in
a normal tone, but it carried all the weight in the world. At this, Willow snapped.

"What about him? You're not meant to be here! You're meant to go back to Apollodorus
Academy. You're meant to forget I ever existed, like Finn did with Autumn." Willow had always thought of herself like Finn until the words flew out of her mouth. She had always imagined she'd grow up and have a happy ending. An ending where she could spend her moments looking at flowers on the sidewalks or baking cookies. It was looking more likely that that ending would be dealt to Griffin. She would be given Autumn's: an ending of endless searching for everything she could never have.

But, Willow had never learned Autumn's full story. She had judged it all on a letter. A piece of a story. A moment.

Griffin paused for one second. One moment.

"I chose to be here, Willow. You've made it quite clear that you don't want me here, but you need me, and I know that." Griffin's voice was stern. Why did it have to be that he chose to follow someone who didn't want him?

"I don't need you." Willow's voice was cold.

It carried the brisk winds of winter and it's harsh snow on its back.

Griffin was unsure why he didn't leave then.

Maybe it was because so many things had happened at once. Immediately after Willow's voice, the sound of a car came up next to them, drowning out Griffin's thoughts.

It was a bright yellow... taxi. Wood Creek was a small town. Griffin knew that much from his short visit. Taxis simply didn't come to Wood Creek. There was no one to pick up, and nobody to drop off. At least, that's what Griffin had heard from Willow. But, one look at her, and he remembered her obliviousness to the world changing around her. He remembered how much of it she *didn't* see.

One look around Wood Creek, and Griffin saw why the taxi was there. He had only ever seen what Willow had shown him. He hadn't seen the second stories stacked on top of the buildings Willow had described to him. He hadn't seen the small stores that had sprouted up like the flowers on the sidewalk.

Willow looked stunned for a moment at the taxi before opening the door. She brushed off the occurrence. It was probably just a one time thing. Willow promised herself she wouldn't see another taxi in Wood Creek.

"Hello!" Willow said once she got in the taxi. It was obvious to Griffin that she was trying to pretend nothing had happened. "Can we go to Ardsas Station, please?" Griffin slid into the seat next to Willow and closed the taxi door. He had no idea why Willow had set their track to Ardsas Station instead of Walt City, and he had no idea why he hopped on the taxi.

Griffin expected the driver to be skeptical of two fourteen year olds asking to drive the fairly long trip, but they made no objection.

"What's your name?" Griffin asked the driver. He didn't think it was such a strange question, but Willow looked at him like he had grown an extra head.

"You can call me Mr. Ellis!" Mr. Ellis seemed pleased that Griffin had asked his name. Griffin knew that often the passengers would put up the plastic dividers and take their ride in silence. They put up dividers that blocked a million opportunities. Cab drivers had been everywhere, and they had seen everything. They dealt with all sorts of people. Griffin had a certain admiration for them.

"Have you ever been to Walt City, Mr. Ellis?" Griffin asked. Mr. Ellis was silent for a few moments. Griffin wondered if he was just ignoring him, but then the man began to speak.

"Yeah. Yeah, tons of times. Just trying to remember the last time I was there." He paused. "I think it was last Saturday. I was driving some folks back after I drove them to Walt City for Thanksgiving. There was some concert there, I remember. Dozens of people were asking for a drive." Griffin nodded in response, mentally scolding himself when he remembered Mr. Ellis was looking ahead at the road.

The way Mr. Ellis looked ahead and the way that Willow looked ahead were very different. Willow looked ahead with no intentions of ever stepping foot in the places she had traveled. Mr. Ellis looked ahead, remembering his time in every place so that he could always go back.

Griffin decided to continue the conversation, and it lasted for most of the drive. Hours were passed with stories from cities that Griffin had always heard of. "The Suitcase Incident," as Mr. Ellis dubbed it, in Rederville, the holiday parties in Worton. The list went on. The longer it got, the more infuriated Willow became. How could all of society go on pretending that its cities were wonderful? Willow was sure that Mr. Ellis hadn't seen the reality of society. He couldn't have seen the tragedies that were awarded to innocence. *But,* Willow thought, *he's seen more than I have.* It was true. Willow refused to believe it. There was no way that corruption could be twisted so far to be loved- and Mr. Ellis talked of his *adventures* with love.

When the taxi finally pulled up in front of the train station, Griffin seemed sad to go. Mr. Ellis reluctantly stopped his stories to say goodbye to the passengers.

"That was one of my more entertaining rides, so thank you." Mr. Ellis said as they exited the doors. "Of course, you can't beat that crew that took a ride home from their wedding after party." Mr. Ellis shook his head, laughing.

As Willow left the taxi, she pulled out the money that she owed Mr. Ellis. The amount was in big black letters on the radio station. Willow pulled out the money and counted out the right amount. It wasn't exact, since she didn't have change.

"Keep the change," she mumbled. Mr. Ellis had kept Griffin occupied long enough so that he didn't pester her about running away from Finn. If Griffin was being honest, he had entirely forgotten what was happening when he was in the taxi. It was only when he saw Willow pull out the money that he *knew* she hadn't had before that he was reminded of the situation.

"Bye, Mr. Ellis!" Griffin waved as the man drove off into the distance, ready to embark on his next adventure.

Griffin walked with Willow over to the entrance to the train station, but he stopped her right outside of the doors.

"Where'd you get the money?" He tried to sound calm, but Griffin had a pretty good idea where it came from.

"Doesn't matter." Willow shoved her shoulder into the door, walking over to the ticket booth. She knew how everything worked now. It was much less magical. "Two tickets to Walt City, please." Willow spoke to a person sitting behind the booth. She handed the amount of money that she knew the tickets cost through the glass, and in return, she was given two tickets. Willow handed one to Griffin without looking at him. She couldn't bear to look at him.

The wait up until the train arrived continued on the same way. They sat in silence, listening to the buzzing chaos of people around them. Griffin picked up pieces of conversation. Some small talk, a few petty arguments, recollections from previous Thanksgivings. It was strange to think that Thanksgiving had only been this past Thursday. It felt like years had passed.

The train that Willow and Griffin had been waiting for pulled into the station and opened its doors. They had both gone on the same journey only days ago. Traveling back and forth as if their destination would appear different when they returned.

Griffin walked through the doors behind Willow. It was always behind her. He was always trying to catch up to her. Not to beat her, but to be equal to her. It had been that way before Willow decided to go on this adventure. The adventure that changed everything for the worse. Griffin knew Willow had left with good intentions. It seemed as if she was returning with less than she had to begin with.

Griffin asked her again, once they had both sat down in the train. "Where'd you get the money?" She looked up at him.

"You know where." Willow watched out the window as the train started to move. The colors of the outdoors blended, causing her mind to see chaos.

"Why?" Griffin asked softly. She didn't answer. All of her possible answers blended together like the sights outside. Nothing was coherent, nothing was right.

Griffin's seed of resentment had grown. It was rooted in him, the way that trees were rooted into the ground. It was fed and watered by Willow's carelessness and neglect. They had planted the seed together, but it had grown without her. It had grown in spite of her.

And now, she didn't have any reason for taking Finn's money. She didn't have any reason for any of this. It was all just a game to her.

The ticket collector came by to punch the holes in their tickets. She handed one ticket back to each of them, and she carried on throughout the train aisles.

"You need to stop and listen to yourself, Willow!" Griffin found that his voice was raised. "Do you even remember why we left in the first place? Because it seems like you don't! You left to find your imagination, not abandon the world. You left to go on an adventure with me, not leave me behind. You left to be inspired again, not to search for hatred. But you keep doing all of that, and for what?!" Griffin needed an answer this time. He needed one last thing that would convince him to *stay.* Willow looked around her. She knew he was right, but he shouldn't have been there. He wasn't supposed to stay. He was supposed to make her lose whatever faith she had in reality.

"It's not Halloween, Griffin! I can't play pretend anymore. It's just past Thanksgiving, and I'm supposed to be thankful. What do I have to be thankful for?" She surfed through her mind. Through all the things that she had been thankful for before. They were all rusted now. Broken parts and things that could never be whole again. Unlit campfires, a barren wasteland of imagination, a torn up train ticket.

"Me," Griffin spoke softly. He wasn't yelling anymore. Willow paused. The only things that her mind had preserved were faces. Faces of everyone she had ever met were still intact. She didn't know most of their names.

"Of course I have you. I always have you. That's the issue."

"What do you mean?" Griffin asked, the frustration from earlier seeping back into his voice. Willow heard it, and she pushed through.

"I always have you, that's the issue. I always have a tether to the real world. Our world. One I can't bear to get rid of. One I don't want to get rid of." She pleaded. Griffin didn't know if she was pleading for him to stay, or leave. He looked at the sign above that flashed to signal its near stop. The train they were on was dropping off something in multiple towns.

The train came to a stop, and Griffin stood up.

"Well I'll be going then, if that's what you want." He let his ticket fall to the ground. "I'll see you later, Willow.

Have fun on your adventure, *Your Majesty*." Griffin walked out the doors, and they closed immediately behind him. Nobody was meant to get off there.

"Wait!" Willow shouted. "Come back!" She ran up to the door, but it was already closed. The little train ticket fell out of her hand and slipped through the crack in the door.

And just like that, Griffin was gone.

Chapter 15

Willow had wondered for years what it would be like to be the Queen of her imagination. She had always thought she would live in a brilliant castle with dragons circling over her kingdom. Everyone would live peacefully, following the example of friendship that Willow and Griffin had set for them.

But, Griffin had gone. There was no friendship to follow anymore. Willow's kingdom would cascade into darkness, fighting against itself until it was nothing but ashes and broken parts.

The rest of the train ride passed in a daze. Willow couldn't think straight. But, the rest of the train had moved on. They had their own lives. Their lives weren't falling apart in front of them.

Willow stepped off the train. She was swallowed by the skyscrapers and the crowds. It hadn't felt so large the first time she had come to Walt City. *Why did everything seem so cheerful?* Willow couldn't comprehend why the sky was such a lovely shade of blue, why choruses of laughter were sounding around her.

There was a screen planted on the side of one of the skyscrapers. Usually commercials of foods and insurance companies flashed across, but they were interrupted by a news channel appearing on the screen. Willow remembered the newspapers she had seen in Finn's attic, and she found herself stopping to listen.

"Hello Walt City!" A female reporter spoke enthusiastically.

"Hello Walt City, and hello Erin." A male reporter addressed the female reporter. "Do you have any news for us today?" He asked, turning to listen to the report.

"Yes, I do, Derek. We have word this morning from Wood Creek about a recent missing person case. A suspect has been taken into holding, but we'll be getting back to you with more information soon." Erin paused before introducing the weathermen. Willow didn't hear any of the forecast over the rushing in her ears.

It was her fault. *She* had driven Griffin away. *She* had decided to hate the world. *She* had decided to leave Finn. It had to be Finn they had in holding. Willow hadn't thought about the consequences of what she had done. She only saw how it would affect her.

And now, she was completely alone.

It was strange, considering she was surrounded by people. Hundreds of people in every direction, and she was alone.

The world hadn't abandoned her, she had abandoned the world. She had given up hope on everything and everyone she loved. Not even the street signs on every block of the city could help her navigate the chaos of the twists and turns that bent and curved in her mind.

Willow stared ahead at the city. The people she had thought were boring and lifeless. The people who went to work were the same every day. She had turned into them. She had become so focused on finding her imagination that she forgot what she had. Willow had turned a blind eye to everything she loved, and while she was looking away they all disappeared.

She had missed all the moments. Ms. Rosen's croissant, Finn's feast, Griffin singing. Willow had taken them for granted. If she had more *time*, maybe she would have appreciated them. It seemed as if time had decided to tumble downhill. Time had accidentally sped up, and everything bad that would ever happen in Willow's life happened right then.

She liked to think that this would be the worst of it, but it wouldn't get better. Not until Griffin was back, Finn was okay, and her life was back to *normal*.

Only yesterday the most important thing to Willow was getting her imagination back. She had wanted Griffin to leave, Finn to vanish from her life, and for her life to go back to what it was before.

Willow's normal was constantly changing.

Sometimes it changed for the better, sometimes for the worse. Change was like the campfires they had at Apollodorus Academy. All it took was one spark that flew loose, one thread out of place, for the fire to spread into the trees. Willow had to be actively trying to stop change in its tracks in order for everything to remain the same. But, stopping the change took longer than accepting it. Willow couldn't afford that time.

When she was younger, Willow hadn't known about time. She hadn't known how to read

a clock. Willow was free to imagine and play. Then the numbers started piling up with long words, forgotten dreams, and destruction. Willow ignored them. She sheltered herself and left the world on its own.

It was time for Willow to finally look. It was time for her to see what was sitting in front of her. It was time for her life to change. She didn't know which way the change would go, but it was inevitable.

And, as Willow decided on her verdict, a dragon flew across her mind, surrounded by a golden sunrise.

Chapter 16

Griffin paced aimlessly around the deck of the train station. He had gotten off in his blind rage. It scared him now that his raw emotions would produce such a reaction. It scared him that quitting was his immediate decision when it was left solely to impulse.

He had stuck around for so long. Griffin had endured the entire adventure, and for what? Just to quit? He had his doubts about the whole situation he and Willow had gotten themselves into, but everything he had done would be worth nothing if he didn't keep going. Quitting would be the easy thing to do. He could probably quit and forget that everything had happened. The only issue was that Griffin knew he would never forget. He would keep wondering if he could've done something different. Every time he saw a campfire, every time he saw a dragon, every time he saw something that would remind him of Willow he would wonder.

Griffin wanted Willow back. It was selfish, he knew. He just wanted his friend back. Griffin knew that they wouldn't be the same, that even if Willow found herself again a part of her would stay behind. But, different had never meant bad to Willow and Griffin. As long as they were still friends, they celebrated the changes that they experienced. Because their friendship had always been a constant.

Griffin hadn't realized that any time had passed until he heard the blaring of a train as it slowed down. A few groups of people stood up to board the train while the others sat, still looking down at their phones.

Griffin took a deep breath and considered his options. He could either hop the train or ask someone for a ticket. A small part of his brain screamed to hop the train, but the rational part knew the adrenaline wasn't worth risking everything. Instead, Griffin walked over to a lone person who was lingering around the edge of the platform.

"Hello. Um," Griffin paused before continuing, doubting his decision. "Um, is it at all possible that you have an extra ticket? Or rather, money for an extra ticket? It's totally fine if you don't. You know, it was a stupid question to ask, I'm so sorry for bothering you." Griffin began to ramble, but the person interrupted him with a deep, hearty laugh.

"No need to apologize, son. I'm sorry to say I don't have any extra money at the moment, but you see that family there?" The man pointed over to a cluster of people. Griffin nodded. "I exchanged some pleasantries with them when I first got here. I don't doubt that they would be happy to give you a ticket." The man smiled down at Griffin.

"Oh, thank you so much. I really appreciate your help!" Griffin thanked him as he sprinted over to the family that the man had pointed to.

One of the parents was coaxing a toddler into the stroller, and the other was watching in amusement. Griffin felt bad about interrupting their moment, but the train was at a stop, and it could leave any moment.

"Excuse me, I'm so sorry to interrupt, but I was talking with the man over there, and he said you might have extra money for a ticket?" Griffin sacked his question so fast that the words blended together. He was surprised when the parent that was tending to the toddler shot a sweet smile at him.

"I'm sure we could spare some money. Leo?"

The parent consulted the other. Leo nodded in agreement, his dark eyes lighting up at the chance to help someone out.

"Yeah. I've got it, James. You just handle Ellie." James went back to putting Ellie in the stroller while Leo reached into his pocket. "So, where are you going?" Leo asked Griffin as he counted money.

"Um, Walt City. Thank you so much."

Griffin was stunned that they would give him the money. Leo furrowed his brow in focus as he counted the money. His face relaxed once he had finished, and he held the money out to Griffin in his outstretched arm.

"No problem. That should be enough to get you to Walt City." Leo slapped the money into Griffin's hands proudly. Griffin fumbled with his words as he searched for the words to thank them.

"Good luck on your trip," James said as he and Leo walked towards the train with Ellie.

Griffin stood by himself for a moment before sprinting off to the ticket booth.

"Walt City, please." Griffin said, out of breath. The person behind the stand raised an eyebrow with a glance towards the train, but took Griffin's money in exchange for a ticket.

"You'd better run, don't want to miss it." The person said as Griffin left. He ran through the train's open doors, ecstatic that they hadn't yet closed. It had been hard enough to decide to keep going. If the train closed, Griffin wondered if he would've given up.

Chapter 17

Willow had found her way to a park bench, and she sat there, stunned. The world around her seemed to spin, twisting and morphing until it was an unrecognizable image. She sat up frantically. She needed to get back to Griffin, back to Finn, back to her life.

As she stood, she felt a warm feeling wash over her, making her legs heavy. The buildings around her turned to rocky mountains. The warmth was the comforting heat she felt when she sat in her room, on the window sill, letting the sun wash over her. She wanted to stay, but she knew that her arms were tingling from the cold in real life, that Finn was being held captive, that Griffin was alone. If Willow wanted to feel the comfort of the *real* warmth again, she had to get back. Willow tumbled in front of the bench and immediately moved forwards, panting. She heard the booming speakers from the screen yet again.

"Well Erin we now have a picture of the missing teens. If anyone sees them, please call this number." Willow recognized the voice as Derek.

A photo of the polaroid she and Griffin took only last year was on the screen. Immediately all heads instinctively started turning around in search of the two of them. Willow made a mad dash, running through the crowd of people with a hood pulled tightly over her head. She could hear yells, all along the lines of "Hey! I'm walking here" but she wouldn't dare stop to apologize. As she rushed through the streets she found herself noticing more and more about the people around her. A couple held hands in the streets. One of them wrapped their fingers around a small ring behind their back and started to get down on one knee. There was a mother in a colourful dress holding her child in the sky, spinning around as he laughed. A business man stooped down to pat a scrappy looking dog, giving it a bite of his morning sandwich.

Willow had always called the city folk lifeless people, who knew nothing of fantasy. She hadn't realized that in their own way, they were making her fantasy of hope and peace a reality, step by step. Willow found herself in the central park of the city, her legs were tired from all the running she just did. She figured she was far enough from the plaza of the city to catch a couple of breaths. She slumped against a tree, panting.

Willow lay there, against the tree, observing the people while staying invisible to them. Among the people, she hadn't expected to see a head of brown hair stumbling blindly through the crowds.

"Griffin?" Willow said, barely audible. It seemed as if Griffin had heard her, though he obviously couldn't have. He turned her way, and they made eye contact. Griffin began to bee-line towards Willow, but she stayed perfectly still. She abandoned her trials of remaining invisible as she stood in the middle of the path.

"I'm so sorry." They both said at the exact time once Griffin had come over. Willow choked out a laugh.

"I'm so sorry, Griffin." Willow said, stunning Griffin with the emotion that weighed down in her voice. Ever since the adventure had started, it seemed as if Willow had been trying to hide the emotion from her voice. She hadn't wanted to be vulnerable, but it had made her more vulnerable to live without emotions. It had made her more vulnerable to turn her back on them because then the emotions sneaked up on her. Willow could live with them by her side.

The sun had begun to set, and Willow told Griffin of all that had happened. He knew about Finn and that they were both being looked for. The conversation had flown naturally, but it seemed as if something was strained in their words. It worked like a flowing river with a dam in the center. They had ended up back where they had started, lying on the grassy floor of the city park. Something was different this time.

Willow tried to push the regret out of her head. She stared into the sky. For the first time, the stars seemed out of reach. They used to be diamonds embedded in the deep blue blanket of space. Something she could grab and mold into a song, into a story. Now? They were simply stars, a shine that was thousands of lightyears away. Some of them had exploded many years ago, and this light? Well, It was just a temporary grave. She sighed contently, simply stars. The simplicity of it all didn't make her feel excited like that diamond embedded blanket, she felt more small, more at peace. She was only a speck, and for some reason, she liked that.

Maybe it was because she thought that her choices had little meaning if she was so microscopic. It was a selfish thought, though she hadn't realized that at the time. Every decision was a ripple, every word was a raindrop. Though what she does might not hurt the world, it would hurt her world, her imperfect paradise. She didn't think, she just looked.

Deep down, Willow knew it wasn't the city that drew her and Griffin apart. She wanted so badly to just *look* at the city and blame everything bad that had happened on it. But buildings, businesses and bypassers couldn't destroy their bond. She knew it was her fault. She knew it was the false identity she had tried to mold herself into.

The old Willow would have images and stories of far places filling her mind constantly. Now criticism, hate, and anxiety had taken over, replacing all things she found comforting. But, the criticism, hate, and anxiety made new images in her mind. More realistic images, but images nonetheless. Willow listened to the silence. All she could do was listen, she let herself be engulfed by nothing.

Willow let her drowsiness take over and drifted off to sleep. The stars that were branded in her mind morphed into the campfires from Apollodorus Academy. It flickered high, bright with light.

When Willow woke up the next morning, Griffin was still asleep. It brought some normality back to her life. Some memories of Apollodorus Academy.

She could recall last night's stars. She let herself be wrapped in the memory of them. The world was beautiful, she just hadn't seen it. Outside, the sky was grey. She knew that sky, she knew that was her safe place. Willow went back to a couple of days ago. The time had felt so long ago that she was surprised it didn't come back to her memory sooner. She had been sitting outside, in that weather. Her favorite weather. As the sun rose she tried to let her voice fill the valley, fighting against the wind.

She had wanted to sing the day into life, but words wouldn't come to her. She hoped that opportunity would be there again someday. Willow realized how much her recent and old experiences clashed, not too long ago she wanted the world to be engulfed in her. Last night she had wanted to be engulfed by the world.

Willow and Griffin waded through the sea of people once they had both pulled themselves off of the park turf. It was probably 9 in the morning. Willow didn't know exactly, and she didn't see Griffin's watch present on his wrist.

"Where are we going anyway?" She asked Griffin.

"Honestly? I have no idea. I guess, we're just trying to make our way back downtown." He shrugged.

Willow felt too immersed into the lifestyle of the soulless zombies she had seen all day, and it made her uncomfortable. People disappeared behind buildings. Their faces were erased from her mind as quickly as they came into the picture. Was she another faceless soul? Had she let herself be controlled by the one thing she feared most? Well, she wasn't sure what it was she feared, the reality, the society, the concept, the change, it was all so new. Vulnerable. Willow was completely and utterly vulnerable to the world. Willow knew that was what she had to be.

As they made their way through the city, Willow and Griffin heard screams. A couple of blocks down someone was running through the street with a small box. Willow saw a couple of dollars fall out of it. Behind them a girl ran, yelling.

"Stop! Get back here!" Willow was frozen, unsure of what to do. Griffin immediately jumped into action with an authority that Willow marveled at.

As the thief ran past them, Griffin took the closest nearby object and threw it in front of them on the ground. The thief tripped over it with the utmost grace and fell face first. Money sprawled out onto the street. Willow found herself running in front of the money to stop the thief's hands from grabbing for the dollar bills. The same screaming girl Willow had seen earlier was now in front of her.

"Oh my god, thank you so much!" The girl panted. She had darker skin with a messy braid down her back. Her hair was black, and she had dark brown eyes. Willow and the girl were the same height, but they definitely were not the same age.

"I'm so sorry about that." Willow said, handing her the money box and the money from off of the floor.

"No, thank you! Seriously, if there's any way to repay you, please tell me." The girl said to Willow and Griffin with a contagious enthusiasm.

"Well, I'm sure we can figure something out," Willow joked.

"I'm Griffin. This is Willow. And your name is?" Griffin prompted.

"Bay-Jen. I made it up myself!" Bay-Jen said proudly. "Well, my girlfriend helped too."

As if on cue, a red headed girl rushed up to them. She had brown eyes that seemed to turn green with the sun. Her hair bounced on her shoulders as she ran, and she wore a shirt that was stained with various paints.

"Oh my god, you are a lifesaver!" She exclaimed.

"That's her! Willow and Griffin, meet Iris." Bay-Jen said, handing Iris the money box. Bay-Jen glanced at Willow and Griffin.

"Hi!" Iris said sheepishly as realized she looked a little discombobulated and patted down her shirt and hair.

"What do you sell?" Willow asked. It was a money box, so she assumed it was from a stand.

"Oh! Sculptures. And paintings. And drawings! On this corner! Always good business around this area," Iris said happily. Seeing she had just nearly been robbed, she was acting extremely positive. A little too positive for Willow. A voice inside Willow's head told her to shut up and realize not everything is negative, and being saved from losing all your money is a pretty big thing to be happy about. She didn't know where that voice had come from, she only knew of her voice in her head. Her voice that used to tell tales for hours and now only seemed to drone on and on about problems. Maybe she was her own enemy, was it possible she caused her own distress, her own chaos? *This is not the time for thoughts like those*, she repeated that in her head until she was drawn out of the endlessness of her own mind.

As she snapped back to reality, she heard Iris laughing with Griffin. Bay-Jen's soft laugh blended into the chorus.

"I love these sculptures." Willow marveled at the pieces of art that were messily organized on the stand. "How did you do all of these?" Willow's eyes scanned delicately over the intricate details on every piece.

"Just watching people." Iris smiled at the compliments. "There's an art to people watching. I'd like to master it some day." Iris paused, staring out into the sea of citizens, mingling down the roads.

Looking back at Willow, Iris asked, "Where are you two planning on going?"

"We don't know," Willow said at the same time Griffin said, "Downtown." Griffin and Willow shared a glance.

"So... you're not from here," Bay-Jen clarified. Willow nodded, and Griffin looked down, embarrassed.

"Well, you're in luck. Iris and I can be your personal tour guides!" Bay-Jen exclaimed.

"You would do that?" Willow asked. She found it hard to believe that two strangers they just met would offer to help them out. It seemed as if the world was trying to prove itself to Willow. Griffin was contemplating the offer, more familiar with the true imperfections of the world.

"Of course! We owe you, remember?" Iris agreed.

"Thank you so much!" Willow exclaimed, without a second thought.

"Wait, sorry. Willow, may I speak to you for a moment?" Griffin pulled Willow aside, and Willow waved at the couple as she was pulled away from them.

"Willow, I'm not sure we should do this." Griffin whispered forcefully.

"Why not? They are perfectly nice!" Willow added. "Plus, we have nowhere else to go!"

"But we can't just leave with two young adults we don't even know! This isn't your small town, Willow. This is the big city," Griffin whispered.

"Do you have any better ideas? We can't live on the streets again," Willow snapped, not wanting to pass up the opportunity. "We're all in now. There's no going back, no turning around. We can only go forward. And I think forward for us now is staying with Bay-Jen and Iris." Griffin sighed, weighing their options. Sleep on a park bench, hungry? Or go with two complete strangers who may or may not be serial killers.

"I'm going to take my chances with Bay-Jen and Iris, Griffin." Willow continued.

"Fine. I'll come. But if there are any clues that they are secretly murderers, I'm leaving," Griffin agreed, only half joking.

"Great!" Willow exclaimed, and she ran back over to Bay-Jen and Iris. "We're in!" Griffin and Willow followed Bay-Jen and Iris to their apartment. The group walked up the stairs, and Bay-Jen unlocked the door, revealing what appeared to be a two bedroom apartment. It had one bathroom, a living room, and a small kitchen.

"I love your apartment." Willow said.

"Thanks! We decorated it ourselves!"

"Don't you guys go to school? How do you work and afford all of this?" Griffin sounded like an interrogator. Willow gave him a look.

"Sorry about him," Willow said. Griffin looked shocked. Was Willow waging a war against him? When had they ever not been on the same side? Griffin reminded himself that things were changing. Things *had* changed. Willow hadn't said anything wrong, only stopped him from immediately judging Bay-Jen and Iris. They really did seem like wonderful people.

"It's okay! To answer your questions, we do go to school. We go to an online art school. And we usually work in the afternoons. We aren't... close with our parents. To say the least. But they paid for this apartment." Bay-Jen explained, glancing at Iris when she said the last part.

"It's okay. I'm not close with my parents either." Willow said. They put their stuff down, and they sat down in their living room.

"Want to order lunch?" Iris asked.

"It's my turn to pick!" Bay-Jen exclaimed. Iris raised her eyebrows at her. "But since you two are guests, you can pick our take out tonight."

After the four of them ordered lunch, Bay-Jen and Iris headed out to grab the food. Willow and Griffin sat on the couch in awkward silence, the room filled with tension. Willow still felt guilty about stealing from Finn. The voices in her head had been debating it all day. She never paid much attention in ethics class, but she knew that what she did was not ethical. As her morals changed, she changed. Willow's morals used to be opaque and clear, but they had slowly been engulfed by a new misty reality. She didn't know boundaries anymore. She didn't know herself anymore. Now it had become routine to push her feelings and thoughts deep down, out of sight, out of mind. She felt like an ostrich, sticking her head in the ground to avoid a predator when really, she had just made herself more vulnerable to these intrusive feelings. Griffin was back, though. They watched each other's backs. Willow would never be entirely vulnerable if Griffin was still there.

If that's all Willow could get, she would take it.

Chapter 18

Bay-Jen and Iris came back into the apartment with four large pizza pies in hand. The two of them were laughing, and Iris kept shooting loving glances towards Bay-Jen.

"Right," Bay-Jen said, composing herself for Willow and Griffin's sake. "We got a little bit extra-" Iris burst out laughing in the middle of Bay-Jen's sentence.

"Bay-Jen couldn't decide what kind of pizza to get, and we forgot to ask you two what you wanted. We got every kind that they would let us get in each pie." Iris opened up the boxes of pizza on the backbones of the couch, showing the pizzas to Griffin and Willow. Hand in hand, she and Bay-Jen sat on the couch, holding back fits of laughter.

"Wow." Griffin chuckled, leaning in closer to the box. Willow caught sight of the selection, and soon, all four of them were laughing on the couch.

"Well, don't be shy! Grab a piece!" Iris reached blindly back towards the pizza, steadying the box with one hand. With the other, she pulled out a mystery slice. "Interesting. I don't think I've seen this one before." Iris contorted her face into an overly thoughtful expression before taking a bite.

For some reason, Bay-Jen and Iris made Willow feel calm. They had the freedom to express themselves like Willow and Griffin did, yet they were adults. They were exactly how Willow had wanted to be when she grew up.

"Well that was interesting." Iris remarked after taking a bite of the pizza. She offered the rest to Bay-Jen, who gladly accepted.

"That's one word for it!" Bay-Jen choked out after taking a bite. Willow found herself laughing for the second time that meal.

"Mm." Iris reached for the remote to the television on the table in front of the four of them. "Telly time!" She exclaimed, clicking the on button.

"Nobody calls it that." Bay-Jen laughed. Iris pouted as the TV lit up with the familiar logo.

"Well I think that everyone should call it that!" Willow contributed, happy for the playful conversation.

Griffin hadn't regretted his choice to come back to Willow. He regretted leaving her, but coming back to her was something that he could never regret. Not when he saw the smile spread across her face, talking to two artists who were bound to inspire her. If Griffin knew Willow at all, he knew that she had already developed a love for the two adults.

"Well Erin, it seems as if we have more information on the two teenagers. In addition to the pictures we were given earlier today, we have been given permission to release the story of their disappearance." The TV had finally turned on, but it was Derek, the news reporter, speaking again. Willow paled as her and Griffin's photos were shown on the screen. Iris and Bay-Jen froze with pizza in their hands.

"Griffin Rivers and Willow Fallon are both fourteen years old and attending Apollodorus Academy. They disappeared from Apollodorus Academy on the day after they returned from Thanksgiving break. They've been gone for approximately five days. We are unaware of their current whereabouts, but if you're anywhere near Apollodorus Academy, please be on the lookout." Derek finished talking, and Iris clicked the off button for the TV.

"That's you?" Iris confirmed, her voice soft. Willow gave a slight nod, though she was still staring into the depths of the black screen. Griffin looked Iris in the eye as he tried to determine what was going through her mind. "Do you want to go back? To 'Apollodorus Academy'?" Willow took a shaky breath before answering.

"Yes. Yeah, I do. We do. Not quite yet, though?" She phrased the last part like it was a question, looking to Griffin for support. He gave a crescent of a smile in return.

"Well, you can stay here as long as you'd like." Bay-Jen spoke confidently. "We've run away a few times," Bay-Jen muttered under her breath, earning a playful elbow in the side from Iris.

"Bay-Jen, we're supposed to be responsible adults!" Iris said amusedly, causing Bay-Jen to start laughing, despite the situation they just learned of. The tension in the air was cut, and Willow was eternally grateful.

Bay-Jen and Iris were the cool relatives that Willow had always wished she could've had. Relatives who, instead of trying to suppress her creativity, welcomed it with open arms. They were able to endure Willow and Griffin's plots and schemes, and they even seemed to be helping out. In Willow's mind, Bay-Jen and Iris were more responsible than her family had ever been.

"Thank you guys," Griffin said, receiving wide smiles from Bay-Jen and Iris both.

"Well, that must've been exhausting for you both. Let's just turn on some TV then. None of that news station. I bet all four of us could use a day off," Iris said kindly, clicking the TV back on.

They watched until the sun set, laughing, crying, fighting over the remote. The genres ranged from fantasy to historical fiction, from romance to horror. They each had different tastes in entertainment, which made watching a thousand times more interesting. There was no need to order dinner seeing as the boxes of pizza were still being eaten.

Willow was deeply engrossed in the fourth *Harry Potter* movie- it had been Griffin's choice. Iris tapped her on the shoulder, slightly startling Willow, with a gesture that meant for Willow to follow her outside.

Iris took Willow out to the balcony of their small apartment, and they sat there side by side. The stars shone bright yet again, a strange sight for a light polluted city. The streets hummed with energy, but up on floor 23, things were more peaceful. Iris leaned against the balcony railing. She had stains on her shirt from her morning at work.

Willow wondered if Iris ever felt bad about her career, but Willow thought she didn't. Iris was aware of things most people weren't. She was aware of the fleeting pleasures in life, she was aware of her own family's wrongdoings, of their lies. She was aware of everything, yet she seemed so content. The most content people Willow had seen before Iris were completely oblivious.

Willow remembered *The Giver*, the book about how one person had to remember all of history for their entire nation. That person had to live the happiness, sorrow and pain from a forgotten past. How could someone so aware of everyone's hardships be happy? Willow used to think that it was impossible. That had been the reason she left Apollodorus Academy in the first place.

Iris' eyes gleamed with the cheap ceiling lights as she turned from the balcony to race up the neighboring flight of stairs. Her eyes gleamed like the city floor, but in a more comforting way. A light that Willow could stare into forever, rather than a loud white that Willow always tried to run from.

Willow found some sort of hope in Iris. The same hope she felt when she had first started her venture out into the city. The hope that had dissipated the second she had stepped foot inside the border of reality. The hope she had lost all faith in. Iris interrupted her train of thought.

"Hey, any chance you want to go up to the roof?"

"There's an entrance to the roof?" Willow asked. Iris chuckled.

"There sure is! You can see the whole city from up there." Iris grabbed her hand and pulled Willow through the roof entrance. The roof of the building was dotted with canvases. Some were blank, some painted with beautiful colors. Iris's works were amazing. They were so realistic, yet so fantastical. It was much more beautiful than something that could actually exist in their world, but it did. That must be the secret to her art. It felt like Iris had discovered the secret to her imagination coexisting with reality.

Iris' art reminded Willow slightly of Finn's. Iris' was more advanced, of course, than the childhood drawings Finn had made. But, they both had the same significance to Willow. It was the way that they portrayed the relationship between imagination and reality. It was the way they portrayed the only thing that was totally foreign to Willow. The concept was getting less and less foreign, though.

Iris and Willow let the night wind wash over their faces. The city below them shone, emitting hundreds of various colors of lights. LED signs flashed desperately to get the attention of the people below. The faint sounds of cars, parties, and casinos all clashed, creating a rise in Willow's adrenaline; a deep longing to be down with the life of the party. A lust to be back where she had ruined her friendships, made vital sacrifices and threw away her life. She got chills down her spine. *Why did she want to be back down where she had lost everything?* She had to remind herself that was also where she gained everything back.

Willow finally sat back and let herself be engulfed by reality.

"It's a good place to think," Iris said, her voice sounding like it was part of the soft winds that blew Willow's brown hair.

"Yeah. It is," Willow agreed. She turned her head towards Iris who reached into her pocket and pulled out a pencil and a sticky note.

"Write it down. Whatever you're thinking right now. You'll want it later, when you grow up." Iris put the pencil into Willow's hands. Willow wasn't sure what Iris was getting at, but she found herself trusting the redhead. Willow began to write on the sticky note.

She, who could speak the tongue of mortals but could not see through eyes. Willow knew how existence was in her life. She knew first hand how hard it was to fit into the mold her family had made for her, but she never figured how hard it would be without it. If she hadn't had any mold to run from, she would never have had everything that made her Willow. She never realized that she wasn't alone, which was why this whole thing had become so monotonous, so forced.

She, who seemed to procrastinate her own demise. It had been a long time coming, the fall of her creativity. This was her fate, maybe her destiny. If only she still believed in destiny. Then maybe she wouldn't try so hard to fit the picture she had painted for herself. Willow had put herself into her own bonds while trying to avoid her family's. At first, Willow would've preferred her own, but now, she realized that either way, she wouldn't be free.

She, who could reverse a tsunami in her mind but once she faced one in real life all she could do was cry. She had thought of herself in the city before. She had planned for what never happened. She could fight anything in her head. Willow had fought everything in her head, but once the real monsters came? The monsters of reality, of fear, of despair, even of hope? Once those demons appeared, Willow could only stand and watch as those who she loved perished.

She, who did not live her life but wrote it. She hadn't truly experienced the wonders of the world, she hadn't felt fear, she had never felt exalted. The point was she hadn't felt the terrors that made living bearable. She had only felt her own reality. Her own little paradise with crumbling walls that struggled to protect itself from the outside. Walls that were bound to collapse. Willow had never truly *lived*.

She, who's broken memories turned to poems. She was turning her broken memories into poems, she had made corrupted songs from blooming flowers, she had tried to take over an entire valley with her voice but her reign of terror had stopped. Her power had faded, she was once again down with those who felt more than happiness. She was with those who called themself free while in cages and those who yelled they were trapped while sitting atop the world.

Iris smiled as she read over Willow's shoulder. Willow's words echoed those of a younger Iris from years ago.

She, who was oblivious to all the chaos in her mind that was blocking her ability to remain blind to the outside. She had no power over the outside world. She only had what she held valuable. Only the frantic collapsing of her cynic fantasies. She grasped her fingers around a lie instead of the hands of her allies. She held onto the glimpse of a hope to be back where she was blind from a world that she had deemed dangerous.

She, who once saw her mind as void, endless space. She remembered her lucid dream. Willow remembered her muffled screams. She knew that was only her mind trying to justify the sudden change in routine. That dream where she blamed all of her issues on her parents and reality. Both were far from helpful and loving, but they were definitely not the cause of all her problems.

She, who had dropped the quill on the final line. She was almost there. She had almost found herself. The wispy figure of the dragon in her mind made itself known. Instead of flying over a medieval town, it flew over Walt City. Willow had been with people who could help her and heal her from her own misguidance, but instead, she fell trap to it again. She let herself be fully consumed by the dark void she hated, but that Willow had willingly entered.

She, who had secretly known her own demise. Willow dropped the pencil on the last blank space of the sticky note.

"I'm finished." Willow whispered. Iris smiled encouragingly at her.

"This part's finished. What will you do next?"

Chapter 19

"I need to go back," Willow declared, turning to look Iris in the eyes. Iris smiled sadly.

"I know." Iris led Willow over to the lines of canvases, and Willow was expecting that Iris would show her one of her paintings. Willow had been eager to see one of them up close. But instead, Iris brought her to one of the blank canvases. "Tell me about your imagination. Just talk." For some reason, the words began to flow out of Willow's mouth. Iris pulled out a myriad of colored pencils.

As Willow talked, Iris drew. Soon, the canvas was populated by skyscrapers, people, trains, dragons, the stars, and magic. The moon light doused the painting in it's silver cloak, highlighting the gold of the train ticket in the drawing that Willow hadn't realized she described.

Willow wondered what Iris could've done if she had more time. But, they didn't have any more of that. Willow had wasted enough time hating the world. She wasn't going to sit around and do nothing with the time she had left.

"It's beautiful, Iris," Willow spoke. Iris shook her head modestly.

"You drew it. I only put it down on paper. You should try it some time." Iris stared at the yellow sticky note that Willow still held in her hand. Willow looked at the drawing Iris had made one more time before turning to go back down the stairs to the apartment. Her steps were echoed by Iris's, creating a rhythmic song that brought her back to Griffin singing on the streets.

When Willow and Iris entered the apartment, Bay-Jen and Griffin were both asleep on the couch. The television was still on, and the box of pizza was still open. Iris flopped herself onto the couch next to Bay-Jen, and in a few minutes, Willow could hear her snoring over the sound of the droning television.

She paced along the back of the couch, mindlessly gnawing on a slice of pizza. Willow didn't want to miss anything, any of the moments that she had left. Willow thought back to the dragons that had been her imagination. Her mind seemed so much more than that now. It blended together like the colors of Iris' paintings.

Willow went over to the sliding glass doors that opened up to the balcony, to a whole new world. She didn't open the door. Instead, she looked through the beige tinted window. Willow was a spectator to reality. But where once there was a wall separating the two of them, there was now a door.

To Willow's surprise, Griffin stirred on the couch, waking up. He looked around groggily before spotting Willow. Noticing Bay-Jen and Iris had dozed off on the other side of the couch, Griffin carefully got up and walked over to Willow.

A few of the wooden floorboards creaked, but none loud enough to wake Bay-Jen and Iris from their slumber. Griffin sat down next to Willow. He looked out the window in front of them, seeing the city with his own eyes.

For a moment, they just sat there, staring into the distance. The sound of the TV blended with the horns of cars and the cheering of people down below. But the lights of the city gleamed beautifully. They were scattered around the city. A deconstructed rainbow.

Griffin remembered the challenge that Mx.

Wilde had sent him on. To make people love books. It had been more than that, though. It had been to make people love the stories that the books told. Willow had learned to love stories. Griffin hadn't thought Willow would be the subject of his challenge, but she had been. Even though it had only been one person, Griffin had made a difference in the world.

"We're going back tomorrow," Willow said,

matter-of-factly. Griffin found himself unsurprised by the declaration.

"Yeah. You think they'll let us back in?"

Griffin asked, a hint of worry seeping into his voice. Willow shrugged, trying to appear nonchalant.

"We didn't miss that much of school. Sure, we'll probably have detentions for the rest of the year, but yeah. I think they'll let us back." Willow let out a small laugh. She tried to keep her voice low, not wanting to cause any ripples in the air of the night.

"What about the scholarship?" Griffin questioned. Willow had been thinking about the scholarship. She handed Griffin the yellow sticky note with her poem scrawled across the lines. Griffin read it through quietly, taking in every word and all the words left unsaid. "It's brilliant. They'll like this." Griffin complimented the writing. He knew that it wasn't Willow's usual writing style. When she wrote stories they were fantastical and descriptive. The poem on the sticky note was simple, but real. It was something you could hold. Something you could appreciate, but it still had the contents of Willow's creativity, poured onto a page.

Neither of them wanted to go to bed. The only thing they had left to do was wait for the sun to come up. It's glow would replace the shimmering stars. The bright blue sky would replace the black of night. Instead of constellations, the sky would be populated by clouds. There were stories held in the sky.

The orange hue began to climb into the sky, hiding the stars away. Iris yawned as she got off of the couch, smiling at Willow and Griffin looking out into the city.

"It's pretty, isn't it?" Iris asked, startling Griffin and Willow. She chuckled at their surprise. "Good morning to you too!" Griffin and Willow stood up off of the ground, walking over to Iris.

"Is Bay-Jen still asleep?" Griffin said quietly, not wanting to wake her if she was.

"Oh yeah. But feel free to talk normally. I swear she could sleep through the end of the world." Iris shook her head affectionately.

"Oh, I know a little something about that." Willow looked directly at Griffin. Iris burst out laughing at the playful banter.

"Hey! That's not fair!" Griffin pouted, following Iris over to the kitchen.

"Let's see... we have some cereal, waffles, pancakes, chocolate. What do you two want?" Iris opened the cabinet doors to show Willow and Griffin the selection of breakfast foods.

It hit Willow that this would probably be their last meal before they went back to Apollodorus Academy. They had started the journey with waffles, and that was how Willow wanted to end it.

"Waffles, please." Willow watched as Iris made the waffles. She performed every movement with elegance, even just for the task of making waffles. Willow wanted to know what it was like to watch Iris paint. To watch as she masterfully arranged the colors on the canvas to paint a picture.

"Guess I'm late to the party?" Bay-Jen had woken up and rubbed her eyes tiredly.

"She wakes!" Iris joked, checking on the waffles.

"Iris is making waffles for us," Willow explained, earning a nod from Bay-Jen. Bay-Jen walked over and stood next to Iris by the countertop.

"And after the waffles... are you leaving?" Bay-Jen asked solemnly. Willow and Griffin nodded in unison. Bay-Jen frowned and looked sadly down at the marble patterned counter. "You'll have to come visit us!" she suggested hopefully. Iris chuckled.

"Bay-Jen, I'm sure if they are ever running away from school again and happen to arrive in Walt City, they'll come here." Iris was only half-joking, winking at Griffin and Willow. She compiled all of the waffles on one plate and put it on top of the kitchen counter. "Have at 'em." Iris took a waffle of her own.

"These are a lot better than the cold waffles." Willow directed the statement at Griffin, who let out a laugh. They had come so far from the beginning, yet here they were, still eating waffles side by side. Not much had to change for *everything* to have changed.

Iris and Bay-Jen had no clue what Willow was talking about, but they both laughed along anyways. Willow knew it was one of those moments that she couldn't forget. There was nothing special about it. It was the comfort of laughing around a table. It was as if everything was alright.

Chapter 20

Willow and Griffin stood up, ready to leave.

They had all finished their waffles after small talk and debate about the proper way to eat a waffle.

"It was great to meet you," Griffin offered awkwardly, desperate for something to say. Bay-Jen shook her head vehemently.

"No, it was great to meet you! Here," Bay-Jen ruffled through her pockets. "You'll need this for the ride back." Bay-Jen put money into Griffin's hands. He stared, awestruck at the gesture.

"It's the least we can do!' Iris exclaimed cheerily. Griffin tried to form words, but nothing came out. Willow beat him to it.

"But... we didn't do anything?" She cocked her head, grateful for the gift of the money, but unsure why they received it.

"Sure you did! You stopped that robber, you gave me some new art ideas, and it's always good to have some new faces around the apartment." Iris grinned. Willow had nearly forgotten about the scenario that had brought them together in the first place. It seemed as if it had been a magnificent string of coincidences, all leading up to that very moment where the four of them stood in front of the door.

"I'm sure you're eager to get going." Bay-Jen opened the apartment door to the world. Willow and Griffin walked through with cheeky waves and small smiles back towards Bay-Jen and Iris.

Griffin and Willow were back on their own, navigating the strange maze of Walt City. But this time, they knew the way out. They knew the path out to the end. They had been there and back again. It was a different path, now. A different path, with a different end, but still the same maze. Still the same maze through the city, through their minds.

Willow realized she was walking mindlessly to the subway entrance. The path had engraved itself in her mind, knowing that she'd need it later.

"This way!" She called back to Griffin.

The two of them raced down the staircase into the underground. Willow felt like she was part of the world, buried so far beneath it's weaving.

The two of them quickly paid for a ticket back to the station they had first set off from. It was standard procedure, now. The giving and taking of the world. There were prices for everything. Everything was a decision, whether or not to take the step forward. Sometimes you got the chance to step backwards, and if you didn't take it, it got left behind forever. Sometimes that was a good thing, sometimes it was bad, but there was always a price.

"We're actually going back," Griffin said as he walked onto the subway train. He tried to keep his movements slow and calculated, calm and soft. He was worried that he would startle himself with the notion of punishments when he got back to school. His fate was no longer up to him. It was a leap of hope over the chasm he had already walked across. The tightrope was gone, snapped and fallen into the abyss.

"It's crazy, right?" Willow sounded as jittery as he felt. But, Griffin heard, there was excitement mingled with her fear. Willow was excited for an adventure. Because that's all that life was, wasn't it? An adventure?

Willow and Griffin felt as the subway began to move. They couldn't go back anymore. Walt City was behind them, and Apollodorus Academy was ahead. They were a step away from losing everything or getting their lives back. *But, what would happen if I didn't go back to Apollodorus Academy?* Willow found herself wondering. The possibility that the school would expel them was high. With the added risk of Willow's scholarship, she wasn't sure if she had any control over the choice.

She would miss every detail about Apollodorus Academy. Her dorm room, where the light beamed perfectly onto her bed. The campfire, where so many of her stories had been born, mixing with the flames to bring them to life. Mx. Wilde, the teacher who had stood up for Griffin and Willow when others hadn't.

Then there was Griffin. Willow had been responsible for getting him into trouble with the school. She had taken him on the twisted maze she had mapped out. Willow hadn't considered that Griffin might take the damage for her actions. He had to stay at Apollodorus, even if Willow couldn't. She wouldn't forgive herself if his world came crumbling down because she had come to him.

Willow tried to capture the moment in front of her. It could very well be the last before she and Griffin reached a fork in the road, and they had to choose which way to go. Willow and Griffin would go their separate ways. They would be Autumn and Finn, their friendship stored in a layer of dust somewhere.

"Willow, what ever happened to those dragons?" Griffin asked.

"Don't know." She shrugged. "I let them go free. They're somewhere, living happily, I'd assume." Willow had used to think that her imagination was free. It was her pride that the paints of her imagination splattered freely, but they were confined to the canvas. Art was everywhere, followed by music and stories. And, somewhere in the depths of her brain, Willow knew that the dragons dwelled.

"Good." Griffin spoke. "I'm glad." Griffin thought back to Apollodorus Academy, and started laughing as a thought popped into his mind.

"What?" Willow asked, confused. Griffin kept laughing. "What?!" Griffin kept laughing,

unhearing. Willow joined in, having no clue what was funny.

"Tyler," Griffin barked out, almost in tears from laughter. Willow hadn't spared a thought for Griffin's roommate, but she could only imagine the chaos he had caused.

"According to him we're probably halfway across the world right now," Willow said through fits of laughter. Griffin countered her theory with one of his own. The rest of the ride went on, each theory crazier than the last. It was a nice distraction from the severity of what had actually happened.

When the subway stopped moving and signaled that it was Griffin and Willow's stop, both of them ceased their laughter. They still had time. There was still time. The clocks kept ticking faster. Too fast, or too slow. They narrowed in on the moments, drawing out the good ones and the bad ones, unable to distinguish the difference from the strength of love and hate.

Time could go by. Years could go by. Willow knew that she would never forget any of the moments she had remembered to live. Time couldn't take away the memories she had made. It didn't have the power to erase the past, only to add a future.

Willow and Griffin exchanged nervous grins as they walked out of the subway, reentering the world above ground.

"Let's play a game?" Griffin suggested, though it was more of a question. It was an attempt to break the uneasy tension that stretched through the air.

"Yeah," Willow agreed as they started down the path towards Apollodorus Academy. "Which one?" Willow tried to keep the nerve out of her voice.

"Eye spy?" Griffin couldn't think of any other games. None that they could play while walking, at least. Willow nodded, clutching the yellow sticky note that she had stuck inside her sweater pocket.

The two of them walked the way back, pointing out the pictures of nature. Sometimes the item of their eyes was a lone tree, other times it was a flower, hidden amongst a blanket of rocks and weeds. There were so many more things to see if you just *looked.* Willow had never looked before. She had averted her gaze, refusing to see any of the good in the world. But now, she saw flowers, she saw light, she saw *life.*

Both of them froze when they saw the buildings of Apollodorus Academy peeking out from the top of the trees. The current subject of their game was lost, replaced by the looming buildings. It seemed much scarier on the outside of the campus. Willow feared her home.

"Do you think they are still looking for us?" Willow asked softly.

"Yep. Yeah." Griffin wiped a thumb across his upper lip. "Yeah, definitely. They're probably looking now."

Willow peeked around the corner, catching sight of grown ups flitting around campus. They turned anxiously, hand gestures accenting their emotions. Willow wasn't sure if the subject of their worry was her and Griffin, but if it was, she didn't know how to even start to apologize.

Willow caught sight of Mx. Wilde, standing on the other side of campus. She found herself stepping into the clearing, directly in line with Mx. Wilde. When the teacher looked up, their eyes locked onto Willow's.

"The kids! They're right there!" Mx. Wilde shouted, their voice a collage of every emotion Willow could've imagined. It felt sudden how the adults turned, their eyes snapping onto Willow and Griffin. The adults swarmed over to the teens, somehow leading them back onto campus. There were questions. Lots and lots of questions. But, the questions would come later.

Mx. Wilde hovered over Willow and Griffin once the others had somewhat dispersed.

"What did you two think you were doing?!" Willow and Griffin hung their heads. "You leave with just a note? And then, then, I have to pretend I had no clue what happened to you two! Do you have any idea the trouble you could've gotten me into?!" Mx. Wilde scolded. Their face softened upon noticing the looks on Willow and Griffin's faces. "I'm glad you're okay." They sighed and pinched the bridge of their nose.

"I did what you said," Griffin said meekly, receiving questioning glances from both Mx. Wilde and Willow. "Made someone love stories, I mean." He looked towards Willow, and understanding passed through Mx. Wilde's clouded eyes.

"I'm glad." They paused before laughing. "You certainly went through great lengths to do so!" Mx. Wilde shook their head in amusement.

"Oh, you have no idea!" Griffin joined in on the laughter.

"You should also both know that Finn was released from the police station. We called as soon as you arrived." Mx. Wilde smiled proudly at them. It felt like a weight had been lifted off of Willow's shoulders. She would never be able to make up for everything she had done wrong to Finn. But now, she at least had a chance.

Willow finally felt like she was home. It could be taken away from her at any moment, but that was what made it so wonderful. Willow had moments left, and she was going to remember them.

Chapter 21

"Willow Fallon and Griffin Rivers?" A woman with her hair done up in a tight bun and crescent spectacles sat across from Willow and Griffin at a desk. It was a miracle that Willow and Griffin hadn't ended up in front of the principal before, considering all of the plotting and scheming they had done on campus. The woman peered over her glasses, obviously expecting an answer from Griffin and Willow.

Griffin nodded, but they both stayed silent out of fear that they might misplace a word. The nod was enough for the principal.

"You are aware that you both violated multiple rules of the school? And, you are aware that these violations could very well result in your expulsion from Apollodorus Academy?" Her voice was icy cold, sharp like a dozen icicles. Griffin and Willow nodded.

"But, ma'am—" Willow was cut off by the stony gaze that was sent her way.

"Tell me why I shouldn't expel you right now." She enunciated each word, puncturing the facade of emotions that Willow had carefully put up. "You're both fairly studious. I've spoken with your teachers, and most have expressed that they don't wish to see you expelled. Particularly Mx. Wilde. I don't want to expel you two." The principal looked straight into Willow's eyes. Willow recognized those eyes. They were the unseeing ones. The ones that she had used to look through.

"So don't." Willow said simply. She was taking a risk, but it was the only thing she knew how to do.

"I'm sorry?" The principal turned her head, wondering if she misheard Willow.

"Don't expel us." Willow repeated.

"Willow..." Griffin drifted off.

"Don't expel us. You've spoken with our teachers. Now you're speaking with us. They said not to expel us, and that's what I'm saying now." Willow took a deep breath. "We have a place here at this school. It may not be as important as your place in the school, but that lets you learn from us. You're so focused on teaching us rules and numbers, but you forgot to learn."

"Excuse me?!" The principal's face contorted in fury, but behind it was curiosity. "What could I learn from you? If I'm correct, you two just ran away from school."

"That's right. We learned something, though. Something that you never taught to us."

"Enlighten me." The principal leaned forward, daring Willow to make a wrong move. It was a game, and it was Willow's turn.

Willow slid her yellow sticky note across the desk. The principal looked down and scanned the lines. She didn't look back up.

"I'm going to have a talk with the rest of the board," the principal sighed. "For now, I'll be working on community service for the both of you. You will spend your evenings with Ms. Wyatt in her classroom."

"Thank you." Willow and Griffin moved out of their seats, sensing the tone of dismissal in the principal's voice.

"Willow, please stay here." The principal stopped Willow as she walked through the door.

Willow gestured for Griffin to wait outside.

Turning around slowly, Willow made her way back over to the principal's desk. She heard the soft click as Griffin closed the door behind him.

"As I understand it, your parents are ceasing their payment to the school?" The principal didn't make eye contact, she only fiddled with the adhesive side of the sticky note. Willow nodded in response before realizing she wasn't being looked at.

"Yes." She said softly.

"Do you intend on staying here at Apollodorus Academy?" The principal flipped the sticky note over, focusing her attention on Willow.

"Yes, I do." Willow confirmed. The principal nodded firmly.

"On scholarship, I assume?" The principal waited for the nod of Willow's head. "Submit this. I'll have a word with the admissions office," the principal sighed, handing back the sticky note.

"W-what?" Willow hadn't known what she was expecting, but it wasn't that. The principal nodded and shooed Willow towards the door.

"You heard me. Now, I suggest you go with your friend before I change my mind." The principal looked curiously at the yellow sticky note. "And Willow?" She interrupted Willow before she cracked open the door. "Nice work." Willow walked out the door, leaving the principal back in her office, alone in thought.

"I take it it went well?" Griffin asked, seeing the smile spread across Willow's face. She nodded.

"Yeah. Something like that." Willow couldn't describe the feeling that she had come out with. She had finally made an impact on someone. She had shared her imagination in the way that she had always hoped to. It was appreciated.

"Let's go to the woods. It's been too long." Griffin started off down the hallways. Willow followed. It was the way it should've been before. She was no longer going to the woods to run away from reality. Instead, she was living in one world.

The woods welcomed Willow and Griffin with open arms. The bugs hummed with delight, and the leaves in the trees danced for them, falling to the ground.

Willow had thought long ago that it was the end. She thought that what she had loved was all finished, that her story was over. But, when she looked around, Willow just saw a new story. One that was waiting to be written. It was Willow's turn to fill the canvas. She was so far from the end.

"Someday you will be old enough to start reading fairy tales again."
-C.S Lewis

About the Authors

Paige Saraga is a thirteen year old who lives in Ontario, Canada. She has always had a passion to create and was able to string the stories she made in her head through words. Paige is constantly switching her interests, though writing has always been one of her main passions. She is going to an arts highschool next year where she will specialize in music, specifically vocal. Her family, friends and teachers have supported her throughout the making of this book.

Diana Gaffner is a 13 year old 8th grader who lives in North Carolina. She loves writing and storytelling. Diana is very creative, and she likes playing music and making art. Diana's friends have been a huge help supporting her on her writing journey.

Mia Seshadri is a 12 year old who lives in New York. She loves to make art, play sports, and to write stories. When Mia started writing, it was her friends and teachers that inspired her to keep going with it.

Tallulah Echtenkamp is a 12 year old who lives in New York City. She loves to swim, write stories, and hang out with her friends. Tallulah started stories, and it was her friends, family, and teachers who encouraged her and inspired her to write.

CPSIA information can be obtained
at www.ICGtesting.com
Printed in the USA
LVHW010845100721
692198LV00011B/631